Missing—One Brain!

DON'T MISS THE ANY OF THE
SIXTH-GRADE ALIEN ADVENTURES!

Sixth-Grade Alien

I Shrank My Teacher

Missing—One Brain!

Lunch Swap Disaster

Missing—One Brain!

Previously titled
I Lost My Grandfather's Brain

by 

Illustrated by Glen Mullaly

ALADDIN
NEW YORK LONDON TORONTO SYDNEY NEW DELHI

This book is a work of fiction. Any references to historical events, real people, or real places are used fictitiously. Other names, characters, places, and events are products of the author's imagination, and any resemblance to actual events or places or persons, living or dead, is entirely coincidental.

ALADDIN
An imprint of Simon & Schuster Children's Publishing Division
1230 Avenue of the Americas, New York, New York 10020
This Aladdin hardcover edition August 2020

Previously published in 1999 as *I Lost My Grandfather's Brain*

Also available in an Aladdin paperback edition.

Book designed by Tiara Iandiorio
The illustrations for this book were rendered in a mix of traditional and digital media.
The text of this book was set in Noyh Book.
Manufactured in the United States of America 0620 BVG
2 4 6 8 10 9 7 5 3 1
Library of Congress Control Number 2020935836
ISBN 9781534464841 (hc)
ISBN 9781534464827 (pbk)
ISBN 9781534464834 (eBook)

CONTENTS

Chapter 1: A Letter Home 1
Chapter 2: Security 3
Chapter 3: Insecurities 14
Chapter 4: Alien Assembly 19
Chapter 5: Hevi-Hevi 24
Chapter 6: Tension 32
Chapter 7: Disaster! 41
Chapter 8: Sudden Sunshine 47
Chapter 9: A Terrifying Development 54
Chapter 10: Squambul 63
Chapter 11: Advice 72
Chapter 12: My Brainstorm 76
Chapter 13: The Perils of Love 83
Chapter 14: Terror! 90
Chapter 15: The Brain-napper 94
Chapter 16: Missing Persons 100

Chapter 17: Revelation 109
Chapter 18: Intuition 114
Chapter 19: Reconnection 120
Chapter 20: A Letter Home 128
Chapter 21: A Letter to Earth 132
Disaster on Geembol Seven
Part Three: Through Caverns Vast and Darkness Deep... 137
A Glossary of Alien Terms 147

FOR RYAN AND DANNY,
AND THE REST OF THE CAST OF
I WAS A SIXTH GRADE ALIEN:
STARSHIP TROUPERS INDEED!

CHAPTER 1

[PLESKIT]
A LETTER HOME

FROM: Pleskit Meenom, on the occasionally terrifying Planet Earth
TO: Maktel Geebrit, on the longed-for Planet Hevi-Hevi

Dear Maktel:

I do not think I will ever understand this planet! I thought I was starting to get along in school. I thought I was learning how Earthlings think. I even thought I was starting to understand about being *cool.*

Unfortunately, there has been another . . . incident.

The good news: It was mostly not my fault

that I lost the brain of the Grandfatherly One.

The bad news: It was enough my fault that I still got in a lot of trouble.

Tim was involved again. Unfortunately, during much of the trouble we were barely speaking to each other.

I have discovered that Earthlings handle friendship differently than we do.

Also, they can be very sensitive.

Once again Tim and I have prepared an account of the entire appalling story. You'll find it in the attached files. Some of them are entries from Tim's journal, made during the time when . . . well, when things were difficult between us.

Are you ever going to come to Earth to visit? The place is strange but fascinating. I can almost guarantee you a trip that will be, if nothing else . . . interesting.

Write soon.

Fremmix Bleeblom!

Your pal,

Pleskit

CHAPTER 2

[TIM]
SECURITY

"No! We're not interested!"

I slammed down the phone in disgust.

"Another reporter?" asked my mother with a sigh.

"You got it."

"Offering money?"

I paused. "Yeah."

Mom sighed again. I didn't blame her. Ever since I had made friends with the first alien kid to go to school openly on Earth, we had been bombarded by reporters wanting to buy my story. But I knew Pleskit and his Fatherly One didn't want that kind of publicity.

I knew, too, that you don't sell out a friendship that

way. Mom completely agreed with me about not selling my story to a reporter. But it wasn't easy to keep turning down that money—especially since Mom's job barely paid enough to keep the two of us going.

"Don't worry about it, Tim," she said when she saw my face. "We'll be fine."

She was worried about me worrying about her—which worried me.

Sometimes I wonder how long a circle like that can go on.

That call came on Sunday evening. (Reporters don't seem to worry about things like regular business hours and family time and stuff.)

On Monday morning Mom drove me and my upstairs neighbor Linnsy to school.

"Uh-oh," said Linnsy as my mother dropped us off in front of the building. "Looks like things have gotten weird again."

Since Linnsy is screamingly normal herself, she can spot weird from a mile away. But you didn't have to be normal (something I, personally, have never managed to achieve) to realize something was cooking at school.

Missing—One Brain!

The sight of eight black limousines—not to mention all the men and women wearing sunglasses and dressed in black—was a good clue.

Our school has been very security conscious ever since Pleskit got here, of course. Even so, we hadn't seen this many agents since the day he arrived.

"I wonder what's going on," I said.

Linnsy gave me a "little punchie-wunchie." (That's what she calls it when she socks me on the biceps because she thinks I'm being dippier than usual.) "Wake up, Einstein. Or did you already forget that our class was held hostage by a disguised alien last week?"

"How could I forget? I was the one the alien was looking for!"

"Don't pat yourself on the back too hard, Tim. Mikta-makta-mookta wanted Pleskit, too. It was just that *you* couldn't be found because you were only two inches high. Anyway, the point is, *that's* why all the security. You can't have an incident like that and not expect them to crank up the safety measures. I would think you'd know that from all that stupid science fiction you watch."

I sighed. Linnsy used to be more fun to hang out with.

When we got to the door of the school, a tall woman wearing a security badge that said ELLEN SANCHEZ asked for our names and what class we were in. Then she checked us against a page of photos to make sure we were really who we said we were.

I figured that would be enough. But when she waved us inside, we found another checkpoint. Here we had to step into a metallic-looking blue box about the size of a porta potty.

"What does this thing do?" I asked.

"Complete body scan," replied the guy who was operating it. "Checks to make sure you're not really an alien in disguise. Also makes a record of your DNA so we can identify you in the future if necessary."

I wasn't sure I liked that.

Linnsy went into the box first. The thing hummed and whined for a minute. Then the door popped open. When Linnsy stepped out her eyes were wide, and she was staring straight ahead like some kind of zombie.

"Did it hurt?" I asked anxiously.

She didn't answer.

"Linnsy! Did it hurt?"

She turned to me slowly, moving almost like a robot. *"Ninoo zannet dorko plink plink,"* she said in a weird, high voice.

I felt a surge of horror. "Linnsy! Linnsy, talk to me!"

She burst out laughing. "Glory begonias, Tim, you are *such* a dweeb!"

I heard a couple of kids who had come in behind us start laughing, too. Even the guy operating the scanner was smirking.

Blushing furiously, I stepped into the scanner myself, half hoping it would send me into another dimension or something.

It didn't.

In fact, it didn't do anything very interesting. A flash of light, a tiny hum—so soft you could barely hear it—and then the door opened again.

"That's it?" I asked, feeling disappointed.

"Neener bixbat rigrum dibbles," said the guy operating the machine. "Translation: Welcome to the weird zone."

I rolled my eyes in disgust. Like I was going to fall for that kind of thing twice. Without even looking to see where Linnsy was, I headed for the classroom.

Pleskit was there already—which meant his bodyguard, Robert McNally, was there, too. McNally was sitting in the back of the room, wearing his sunglasses and looking totally cool.

I would like to be like McNally when I grow up.

"Greetings, Earthling!" said Pleskit when he saw me.

"Greetings, O Mighty Purple One," I replied.

We both smiled.

"Oh, look," said Jordan Lynch, who was sitting nearby. "The Dork Society has decided to hold its annual convention in our classroom!"

Brad Kent snickered. Brad laughs at whatever Jordan says, no matter how stupid it is. I don't want to say that Brad is a suck-up, so let's just say that if Jordan were a ship, Brad would be a barnacle.

Jordan is very good looking and very cool. He's also, in my opinion, a total booger. He's been on my case ever since he transferred into our class a couple of years ago, after the fancy private school he used to go to kicked him out for some reason. Some kids have spent a lot of time trying to figure out what he did to get booted like that. My own theory is simple: The teachers got tired of throwing up every time they had to spend a day with him in their rooms. Linnsy gave me a little punchie-wunchie the first time I told her this theory, but personally I think it makes a lot of sense.

The day started with two announcements from our teacher, Ms. Weintraub; one was sad, the other surprising.

The sad news was that we had lost two more kids—Robert Devine and Cissy Jupe—because their parents decided to pull them out of the class after what had happened the week before.

The surprising news was that we were getting two *new* kids—a boy named Larrabe Hicks, and a girl named Brianna Sawyer.

Larrabe seemed nice, but dorky—which meant I might get along with him.

Brianna, on the other hand, seemed like she was from another world altogether—and I don't mean from another planet. She was sophisticated, and, well . . . developed.

That's this weird thing that happens in sixth grade. A few kids start to grow really fast. It's like the hormone fairy comes and taps them on the head one night, and all of a sudden—*sproing!*—they shoot up about six inches in two weeks. The thing is, you never know when it's going to happen. Or where.

Also, I think it happens to more girls than boys. At least, it hasn't happened to me yet. And we have several girls in our class who are taller than most of us guys. Which is not, believe me, the way things used to be.

Jordan is one of the tall guys, of course.

The new kids seemed nice enough, but they were both really interested in Pleskit. That wasn't really a surprise—who wouldn't be interested in an alien? But when I watched them talking to him that day, trying to make friends, I got a strange, unpleasant feeling in my stomach.

I wouldn't have known what was going on inside me if Linnsy hadn't explained it at recess that afternoon.

"You're jealous, Tim."

"Jealous?" I asked in surprise. "Of what? It's not like Pleskit's my girlfriend."

Linnsy gave me a little punchie-wunchie. "If we hadn't been such good friends back in kindergarten, I would just abandon you to the savage forces of natural selection. Let's think this through for a minute. First, you don't have a lot of close friends."

I started to object, but she cut me off.

"It's not like anyone dislikes you, except Jordan, who doesn't count, since he's barely a member of the human race. But there's no one you're really close to, either, since you're basically too weird for real life."

"Thanks, pal."

"I'm not trying to insult you. I'm just here to cash your reality check. Most of the time I actually like the fact that you're kind of weird, except when you act so dorky that you embarrass me. The point is, when Pleskit got here, two things happened. One, we finally had someone in class weirder than you. Two, you guys got to be friends pretty quickly—which was logical, since you were the closest thing we had to an alien already. So it's no surprise that when you see someone like Larrabe or Brianna trying to be friends with Pleskit, it makes you nervous."

"Why nervous?"

"Because, genius, you don't want him to be better friends with someone else than he is with you!"

"That's the stupidest thing I ever heard!" I said. But I only said it because I realized that what Linnsy was talking about was true.

Emotions.

What a stupid idea.

I bet they were invented by a girl.

CHAPTER 3

[PLESKIT]
INSECURITIES

My classmates grumbled about the new security measures several times throughout the morning.

"It's like going to school in prison," said Michael Wu.

"Yeah, well, you know whose fault it is, don't you?" asked Jordan. "You can blame it all on our purple pal, Pleskit."

"Hey, it's not Pleskit's fault," said Tim loyally.

"That's true," said Jordan. "Half the blame goes to you."

Tim started to do his trick of turning red, which is called blushing.

"Why does he get the blame?" asked Brianna.

We were sitting at our desks, doing the morning assignments while Ms. Weintraub worked with a reading group.

Jordan glanced at Ms. Weintraub. She appeared to be totally focused on the group. Lowering his voice, he leaned toward Brianna and started to tell her about what had happened when Tim and I decided to shrink him, and accidentally shrank Ms. Weintraub and Tim instead. Before he could get very far into the story, Ms. Weintraub looked up and said calmly, "Jordan, I think you still have work to do."

Jordan rolled his eyes and settled back in his seat.

When we went outside for recess, the conversation picked up again. I pointed out that one reason the security measures were needed was that Earthlings live in a violent and unstable society.

"Nice try, Plesk-o," said Jordan. "But it wasn't an Earthling who tried to take over the class last week."

This was a distressing observation, mostly because it was true.

The new kids, Larrabe and Brianna, were standing with us. Larrabe was short, one of the shortest kids in the class. He had brown hair and a very serious expression. "Boy, I'm glad I got moved to this class," he said after Jordan had finished telling his version of what happened last week. "I had to plead like crazy with my mother to put my name on the list to get in here if any other kids left." He looked at me shyly and said, "I told her it was a great educational opportunity."

Another distressing observation. I do not wish to be thought of as an "educational opportunity."

"My mother was totally the opposite," said Brianna. She was very pretty, by Earthling standards, with thick black hair, large eyes, and a turned-up nose. "When she found out Dad's company was moving us to the town where Pleskit goes to school, she immediately called the principal and started insisting that I be put in this class. She was the one who thought it was a great opportunity." She glanced at me and smiled. "I just thought it was cool."

McNally was about ten feet away, keeping a close eye on us. I like McNally, and value his protection. Even so, I sometimes wish I could get a little time away from him. To my surprise, he looked unhappy. I slipped away from the group and went to speak with him.

"You are wearing your cranky face, McNally," I said, looking up at him.

A corner of his mouth twitched—not a smile, exactly, but something that looked like it might turn into one, given a lot of work. "Yeah, I probably am."

"Is there a reason for this displeasure?"

He glanced toward the corner of the building, where one of the new security team was standing. "Professional matter," he muttered.

"You do not like the new guards?"

His scowl grew deeper. "I just wish they weren't considered necessary," he said, not speaking much above a whisper.

"Ah," I said, for now I understood the problem. He was taking their presence personally, as if it meant that he had not done his job adequately. I wanted to say something to him but could not think of what it should be—especially since I had dragged him into the crazy shrinking plan to begin with. Then Tim came running over and pulled me off to talk.

When we went back inside, it was time for us to write in our journals, which I enjoy doing. I was reflecting that the day had been acceptable. Not great. Jordan had been annoying, and the aftereffects of last week's events were a little embarrassing. On the other hand, nothing really terrible had happened, which put it ahead of most days since I had arrived on Earth.

Then the principal, Mr. Grand, got on the loudspeaker. With just a few words he changed the day from "acceptable" to "horrifying."

CHAPTER 4

[PLESKIT]
ALIEN ASSEMBLY

Mr. Grand seems to have an affection for say-ing what is obvious. For example, this is how he started his announcement:

"Attention, students! As most of you know, we have the honor of hosting the world's first alien student in one of our sixth-grade classes."

Since everyone in the *world* knew I was going to school here, this struck me as being unnecessary. Anyway, that wasn't the horrifying part of his announcement. This was:

"What you may not have known is that ever since he arrived we have been hoping to have an assembly where you could learn about the customs of the world from which Pleskit comes. His parental unit, Meenom Ventrah, is an extraordinarily busy person. But he has managed to find time in his schedule to speak to us this very afternoon. Pleskit will be joining him on the stage, so this will be a good chance for all of you to see our new student and ask questions of both him and his Fatherly One."

I glanced at Tim. He seemed to think this was a wonderful idea. I did not feel the same way. It did not help matters any when Jordan turned to Brad Kent and said in a whisper loud enough for everyone to hear: "Whoa! Dork City!"

"I think it sounds wonderful," said the new girl, Brianna, brushing a strand of her dark hair back from her face.

Jordan looked startled and sat back in his chair. I wasn't sure, but I thought I actually saw him do that trick Tim sometimes does of turning red. This made me feel slightly better.

About half an hour later I got a call from the office to go down and meet the Fatherly One so I could get ready for the assembly. McNally went, too, of course.

My *clinkus* tightened when I saw that Ms. Buttsman had accompanied the Fatherly One. Ms. Buttsman is the protocol officer that our host government assigned to the embassy after the horrifying experiences of my first week in school. She has all the personal warmth of a Zarkaflian *shlnutberg.* Tim calls her "the Butt." I think of her as "The Dreaded Ms. Buttsman."

She stood beside the Fatherly One holding a formal ceremonial robe, an item of clothing that Jordan refers to as my "official galactic dweeb uniform."

"Greetings, Pleskit," she said with a stiff, icy smile. "I knew you would want to dress appropriately for the occasion, so I brought this along."

"Thank you, Ms. Buttsman." I spoke politely. But with my *sphen-gnut-ksher* I emitted the smell of seventh-level crankiness. I was pleased to see her wrinkle her nose in displeasure.

"I'm so glad you've agreed to do this, Ambassador," said Principal Grand to the Fatherly One. "Learning about life on another planet from genuine aliens will be the ultimate in multiculturalism."

* * *

The assembly was held in the cafeteria. The tables had been folded up and replaced by chairs. The curtain on the stage was open. A podium with a microphone stood in the center of the stage. Seated in a row of chairs behind the podium were Principal Grand, the dreaded Ms. Buttsman, the Fatherly One, and me.

McNally stood behind us—as did four additional security guards. Mr. Grand called the assembly to order and introduced the Fatherly One, Ms. Buttsman, and me. Then he turned the assembly over to the Fatherly One.

Everyone clapped when he came to the podium.

"Children of Earth," said the Fatherly One, raising both hands straight out to his sides. "I bring you greetings from the stars!"

Then he smiled and belched a greeting. Though this is standard for Hevi-Hevians, it still caused an explosion of laughter. Ms. Buttsman groaned and rolled her eyes. "How am I supposed to do my job if that stubborn alien refuses to listen to my advice?" she muttered.

I thought about suggesting that she resign, but decided this was not the time to bring up that idea.

The Fatherly One waited for the room to grow silent. Though I could not see him from behind, I suspect that he was scowling. I know from personal experience that the Fatherly One has a scowl that could stop a charging *herklump*.

"Your principal has invited me to speak to you about life on Hevi-Hevi, and this I am most happy to do. However, I think it would be even better for me to *show* you some things about our planet. For this reason, I have brought with me some images of home." He turned to Mr. Grand. "Could you darken the room, please?"

Mr. Grand got up. A few seconds later the lights went out. According to Tim, usually that doesn't make all that much difference in our cafeteria, which isn't really set up to show movies and stuff, since even when you pull the shades a lot of light leaks in. But they must have installed something new over the windows, because we heard *Zip! Zip! Zip!* and suddenly the room was completely black.

People started to talk and laugh, but before it could get out of control, the voice of the Fatherly One cut across the babble.

"Behold!" he said in tones so loud and clear that everyone fell silent. "Behold the world of Hevi-Hevi!"

CHAPTER 5

[TIM]
HEVI-HEVI

As Meenom spoke a beautiful sphere appeared at the front of the room, floating several feet above the floor.

A big "Oooooh!" rose from the crowd. The sound was repeated over and over as the sphere was replaced by a series of astonishing images. I have no idea how Meenom did it; he had no projector that I could see. But the pictures he showed us (in full 3-D, of course) were so incredibly realistic that when we saw a waterfall, we automatically flinched back, because we expected to get splashed.

Brianna was sitting next to me. "Isn't this exciting?" she whispered.

"Incredible!" I agreed.

After a scenery display that made me want to get on a rocket for Hevi-Hevi right that minute, Mee-nom showed us some of the plants and animals of Hevi-Hevi—not all of them, of course; you couldn't do that any more than you could show all the plants and animals of Earth in a single slide show. But we saw enough to know that they were utterly strange and at the same time oddly similar to the kinds of living things we already knew. He showed us exploding flowers, walking trees (they have a main root that's like a drill), and a vicious-looking crablike creature the size of a rhinoceros that is highly prized for its ability to lay eggs of extraordinary sweetness—though it does so only twice a year.

Next he showed us a waterfarm where they raise blobby purple creatures whose outer skin is peeled off every three months, then used for everything from seat covers to snack food. After that he showed us an airfarm where they cultivate vines that grow purple pods the size of bowling balls. These pods contain a liquid so fiery no one on Hevi-Hevi can stand to drink it. Yet it is exported to 516 different planets, where it is considered a special delicacy.

"One of my main tasks here on Earth," said Meenom, after he had talked about this vine, "is to find some items that *you* can use for trading. Now, let me show you a few of our cities."

The first city he showed was exactly as I had dreamed it would be, a place of soaring purple towers and buildings that were weird yet beautiful. The camera (or whatever had been used to make the images) started by showing a far shot of the city, so we could see its towering skyline. Then it swooped in to reveal the aircars, the bustling streets (thronged by millions of bald purple people!), and the huge statues that seemed to rise from almost every corner.

The next city was utterly different. Here the buildings were low and rugged looking, fitting into the land so perfectly that at first you hardly realized they were there.

The third city was so strange that at first we thought Meenom had made a mistake, for the image he showed was of a vast plain of waving purple grass. He laughed at his little joke, then explained that this city was entirely underground. Then he showed us images of its broad streets and cozy-looking buildings.

"This particular building is a nursery," he said, showing us a rounded structure that looked almost like an egg itself. "In fact, it is the very place where Pleskit was hatched."

That created a stir of giggles that made me a little embarrassed for my friend.

"Because your culture has many unresolved issues regarding biology, Principal Grand has asked me not to go into detail about how reproduction works on Hevi-Hevi. So I will simply tell you that every reproductive unit that contributes an egg is invited to the hatching, where they are given one of the childlings in return. All childlings are assigned at random."

It took a second for this to sink in. "You mean you don't get your own kid back?" cried someone sitting a few rows behind me. A murmur began to rustle through the cafeteria.

"That is correct," said Meenom. "Except in cases of accidental rematch, the childling you receive is not from the egg you contributed. Even if you did receive the product of your own egg, you would not know it."

The image had shifted now, showing dozens of

recently hatched Hevi-Hevians. They were bald, purple, and incredibly cute.

"This system has one great advantage," continued Meenom. "All creatures have a deep, powerful drive to protect and care for their offspring. Therefore, when

any child might be *your* child, when the toddler you pass in the street may be the product of your own genetic material, all children suddenly become more precious. Your society claims to love and value children, and even seems to believe this claim. To an outside observer this is a hilarious bit of self-deception. As a re—"

"Really, Mr. Ventrah!" cried Mr. Grand, jumping to his feet and interrupting. "How can you say such a thing?"

Meenom turned to him. "Did you yourself not tell me that this school was greatly superior to the other schools in your city?"

"Well, yes, but . . ." Mr. Grand's voice trailed off. In the dim light cast by the image of the nursery, he looked uncomfortable.

Meenom spread his hands. "Well, there you go. In a culture that truly values children, it would not be tolerable for one school to be inferior to another. All schools would receive an equal share of resources and be required to meet equally high standards. This is the value of our system." He paused, then added, "To put it more precisely, on Hevi-Hevi there is no such thing as a starving child."

* * *

That was pretty much the end of the assembly. The initial plan had been for Pleskit and Meenom to answer questions, but I think Mr. Grand decided their ideas might be too dangerous.

When he announced that it was time to go back to our rooms, a big crowd of kids surged forward and began swarming around Pleskit. I could see that the mob scene was driving McNally and the other special agents buggy. I tried to push my way in but couldn't get anywhere near Pleskit.

At that moment I did not feel like a best friend at all.

Jordan—who has a genius for noticing people's sensitive spots—picked up on this. In a voice that could have been heard two blocks away, he shouted, "What's the matter, Timmy? Your little purple pal dump you?"

Then he began to laugh.

I tried harder than ever to get near to Pleskit to prove that this wasn't true. But before I could manage it, the agents divided the crowd and McNally hustled Pleskit out, shouting that they had to get back for some official event at the embassy.

"Looks like I was right," sneered Jordan. "You're not such an alien insider after all, Tim."

"Shut up, Jordan!" I said.

He didn't hit me; that wasn't really his way. Besides, he didn't need to. He could tell his comment had struck home.

It wouldn't have hurt so much if I hadn't been afraid it was true.

CHAPTER 6

[PLESKIT]
TENSION

The assembly was very embarrassing. Even worse, I was embarrassed *because* I was embarrassed. That is, I knew it should not be embarrassing. It was a simple presentation of things about our world. But I had already realized that many kids in my class consider it embarrassing to have to do something like that, and I was infected by their discomfort.

Even worse, rather than being able to reconnect with the kids afterward, I got rushed back to the embassy. This was especially frustrating because I wanted to talk to Tim. I could tell people had been surprised when the Fatherly One explained our birthing system, and I wanted to see what Tim thought of it.

The reason I got dragged off was that the Fatherly One had scheduled an afternoon meeting with the ruler of the country in which we have established the embassy. (It is strange, and slightly disturbing, that this planet has so many different governments. Small wonder they have so many conflicts. I seem to remember that sometime in our distant past Hevi-Hevi was divided up in such a way. Even so, it is hard to imagine how a world can make any progress like that.)

This ruler, who is called "the president," was a very pleasant person. The Fatherly One later explained to me that he is chosen not on the basis of his actual qualifications for the job, but by popular election. So it is no surprise that he is able to charm people. Even so, it was interesting to see how McNally and Ms. Buttsman were awed by his presence. He was a person, just like them. So what was the big deal?

The president stayed for the evening meal.

Barvgis, the Fatherly One's round and slimy assistant, joined us. He has been trying to learn Earthling jokes, which he was practicing on the president. The one about the farting elephant clearly upset Ms.

Buttsman. The president, on the other hand, laughed very much. So I think it was probably a good joke.

We had Earthling food—ham (which is flesh from an animal called a pig), underground fruits called potatoes, green sticks known as asparagus—all prepared by an Earthling cook that Ms. Buttsman hired for the occasion.

The meal was good, but I can only eat so much Earthling food at one sitting. So later I went to the kitchen for a snack.

McNally and Barvgis were there already, sitting at the table. They both looked worried.

I wondered why, until I saw Shhh-foop.

Shhh-foop is the being who usually does our cooking. She is normally quite cheerful. Now, however, her orange tentacles were drooping mournfully. "Greetings, Pleskit," she warbled when she saw me.

Her voice was so soft I could scarcely hear it.

"All you all right?" I asked in alarm.

"I fear I am no longer queen of the kitchen," she sang sadly. "I was not allowed to cook for this day's gathering."

At that moment the dreaded Ms. Buttsman came in.

"Still moping around?" she asked sharply when she saw Shhh-foop.

McNally snorted in anger. "I suppose it was your idea not to let Shhh-foop cook today's dinner?" he asked.

"It was a perfectly fine meal," snapped the Butt.

"It was boring," said McNally. "Do you really think the president wants food he could have any day of the year when he comes to the alien embassy? Besides, you should have been more considerate of Shhh-foop."

Ms. Buttsman's eyes flashed and her nostrils grew wide, which gave her a very interesting look. "I am more interested in making sure that things go well than in coddling the feelings of the staff," she said sharply. "And that includes you, Mr. McNally. If you do not like the way I do my job, you might consider putting in for a transfer. I think things would go considerably more smoothly around here if your position was filled with someone who has a better attitude."

"Just keep hopin' and wishin,' lady," said McNally. "Because I'm gonna be here long after you're gone."

This was a great relief to hear. I have come to depend on McNally, and I did not want Ms. Buttsman to drive him away. Turning to me, he added, "I'll be in my room if you need me, Pleskit. Send me a cup of coffee if you get a chance, will you, Shhh-foop?"

I was surprised to hear him say this, since he has found Shhh-foop's attempts to make this Earth beverage quite deplorable. But when I saw the way Shhh-foop perked up and heard her warble, "It will be my pleasure, Just McNally," I understood what he was doing.

Ms. Buttsman sniffed and left the room.

"She is not my favorite Earthling," said Barvgis, who had been eating squirmers while this went on.

"Mine, either," I said.

"I wonder how she's going to get along with Beezle Whompis," added Barvgis, tossing another handful of squirmers into his mouth.

I wondered the same thing myself. Even more, I wondered how *I* was going to get along with Beezle Whompis, who was to be the Fatherly One's new secretary, in place of the evil Mikta-makta-mookta. This was an important question for me, since whoever guards the door of the Fatherly One has a great impact on my life. If the newcomer and I got along, my life would be improved. If we did not, things could get *verplexxim* very quickly!

I decided to speak to the Grandfatherly One about the matter. The Grandfatherly One—or, to be more precise, the brain of the Grandfatherly One, since that is all we have left of him—lives in a large vat. The vat is filled with an electrolyte solution that provides nourishment and upkeep. Mounted on the sides of the vat are a pair of speakers that allow him to express his thoughts. It also has sensors for sight, sound, and smell.

"Greetings, O Venerated One," I said when I entered the darkened room where we keep the brain.

"Greetings, Whippersnapper. Have you seen your Fatherly One lately? When you do, please tell him that I continue to suffer from extreme boredom!"

"Boredom would be an improvement on what I went through today," I replied.

We spent the next several minutes complaining to each other about how unhappy we were, and how unreasonable the Fatherly One was in the way he treated us. It was very satisfying.

"As usual, life has reversed things," said the Grandfatherly One in conclusion. "I would like to get out

into the world, while right now you would prefer to stay home. Therefore, I am stuck at home, and you are forced to go out into the world. I am moved to compose my first poem in our new language:

THE UNIVERSE:
IS QUITE PERVERSE!"

I farted my approval.

"Ah, I miss being able to do that," said the Grandfatherly One. "Now, on to other topics. What do you think of our Ms. Buttsman? Never mind. I'll tell you what I think of her. I think she's trouble."

"She is a dark cloud hanging over the embassy," I replied. "Also, she does not get along with McNally, whom I like."

"That's no surprise. From what you've told me, the two of them are going to mix like *spratzels* and *grakkims*."

I belched the belch of sad acceptance. I realized it was a relief to be talking to the Grandfatherly One, where I could use my full vocabulary. (Even though I was coming close to breaking the Fatherly One's rule about only speaking the language of our hosts so that we can grow more comfortable with it.)

"I predict a long and nasty battle for dominance between McNally and Buttsman," continued the Grandfatherly One. "With you caught in the middle."

"My joy knows no bounds."

"Ah, sarcasm," said the Grandfatherly One happily. "I like that in a youngster. Shows a healthy view of the world. Speaking of views of the world, I would consider it a personal favor if you could figure out how I can get one. I want to get out and experience this planet!"

"I will do my best, O Venerated One."

Little did I realize what a terrible idea this would turn out to be.

I decided to talk to Tim about a device for getting the Grandfatherly One out of the embassy, as Tim seems to have a special skill for planning such capers.

Alas, before I could speak to him at school the next day, disaster erupted.

CHAPTER 7

[TIM]
DISASTER!
(FROM THE JOURNAL OF TIM TOMPKINS)

Today was one of the worst days of my life!

A pure disaster.

When I got to school this morning, everyone was clustered in little groups, talking and laughing. I couldn't break into one right away, so it took me a while to find out what was going on.

When I did, I was appalled. Larrabe was holding a copy of *The National News*, a tabloid paper I personally hate because it is very anti-alien. The headline, written in huge letters, said:

ALIEN BOY HATCHED FROM EGG!

The tone of the article was pretty nasty, and it

stressed the way Hevi-Hevians are different from us, rather than any similarities.

Even worse was the picture of Pleskit that went with it. Actually, it wasn't the picture itself that was disturbing. It was the fact it had been taken right here in school. But since reporters are completely banned from the building, it raised a major question: Namely—*who* took the picture?

When Pleskit and McNally came in a few minutes later, Jordan shouted, "Hey, Pleskit—nice spread in this morning's paper!"

Then he held up his copy of *The National News*.

Pleskit's eyes got wide. His *sphen-gnut-ksher* swiveled around as if it was looking at the paper, too. *"Geezil beedrum!"* he cried. At the same time the *sphen-gnut-ksher* let out an odor something like dead fish mixed with vanilla and motor oil.

"Eeuuuw!" cried several kids, backing away in disgust.

"Let me see that thing!" cried McNally, grabbing the paper from Jordan's hands. He looked angrier than I had ever seen him. He stared at it for a moment. When he threw it to the floor, he looked even angrier than he had before—which I would not have thought was possible. "How did this rag get a photographer in here?" he snarled, speaking as much to himself as to us kids. "This place is sealed up tighter than a drum."

"It could be worse," said Larrabe helpfully. "At least it's not one of those skeezy weekly papers you get at the supermarket, like *The National Scoop.*

"My father calls that one *The National Pooper-scooper,*" said Chris Mellblom.

That wasn't a bad name for it. In the last year *The National Scoop* had announced, among other things, that the president was an alien, that the world was going to end on July 27 (it hadn't), and that Elvis was alive and teaching school in Boulder, Colorado.

None of these was true, of course. (At least, I don't think the president is an alien.) But that doesn't seem to make any difference. I used to love that paper because it was so weird. Then I realized they were just making up their stories, and I decided I hated it.

McNally wasn't the only one who was upset by the article. We had barely settled into our seats when the loudspeaker came on and Principal Grand said, "It has come to my attention that an unpleasant newspaper has acquired a photograph of one of our students—a picture taken in this very school. Out of courtesy to the student, I will not mention his name."

(Like anyone didn't know who it was!)

"However, I must stress that this is not acceptable. Our students are guaranteed privacy and security within these beloved walls. If the person who took this photograph will come and see me privately, we may be able to deal with the situation leniently. If not—well, let me just say that we *will* find out who it was, and when we do, you'll wish you had come to me on your own.

"I trust there will be no repeat of this incident.

"Have a nice day."

Mr. Grand would end an announcement with "Have a nice day" even if had just proclaimed three weeks of detention for every kid in the school.

Ms. Weintraub started to say something, but a knock at the door interrupted her. It swung open, and two guys dressed just like McNally (black suits, dark glasses) stepped into the room.

"Sorry, ma'am," said one of them. "Given the quality of that picture, we think the photo was taken with a high-resolution camera. We need to do a camera check."

Ms. Weintraub hesitated, then nodded and said, "Yes, that's probably a good idea."

I wondered if she thought one of us was the rat.

The guys whipped out a couple of detectors of some sort and began scanning the room.

McNally didn't say anything, but from the look on his face I could tell he was furious. Clearly he considered this room his territory and didn't like these guys barging in.

When they got to me, the first agent bent down to look in my desk. "Good grief, kid," he said, sounding horrified. "How do you ever find anything in there?"

"I've got a system," I said, feeling a little defensive.

"What's it called, 'Cram It and Jam It'?"

I was about to point out that he was here to look for a camera, not to insult defenseless students, when his detector started to beep.

"Gotcha!" he cried.

Thrusting his hand into my desk, he pulled out . . . a camera! I felt cold. Even worse, I began to blush. Not, I want to point out, because I was guilty. But I've had this problem since I was little of blushing whenever something goes wrong, which always makes me *look* guilty.

It didn't help that every eye in the room was turned toward me, staring so hard I felt as if I were naked.

"Come on, kid," said the agent gruffly. "We want to have a little talk with you."

CHAPTER 8

[PLESKIT]
SUDDEN SUNSHINE

I was stunned when Tim was hauled away by the security agents. How could this be? I thought he was my friend. How could I have been so wrong? And how would I ever become a diplomat like the Fatherly One if I did not learn to judge people's motives more clearly? What kind of fool am I?

(Alas, the answer to that final question eventually turned out to be even more disturbing than I first suspected.)

I do not remember what we discussed in class that morning. I could no more concentrate than a *plonkus* can climb a tree.

However, when we took a brief break, I discovered an unexpected side effect of the nasty situation—a pleasant side effect. Suddenly the other kids were very sympathetic to me.

The Grandfatherly One helped me analyze this later. We decided that several things were going on. One, the kids felt sorry for me because I had been betrayed by someone who had seemed to be my friend. Two, they felt a little guilty because their own unconscious fear and prejudice had kept them from being more friendly to me themselves. Three, our classroom—which is, in a way, our home—had been violated, both by the sneak who took the picture and by the agents who came to find him. My fellow students needed to heal the wound, repair the broken wall. And in doing that, they took me in, rather than shut me out.

Chris Mellblom was the first one to come up and speak to me. "Man, that stinks," he said, shaking his head sadly.

"Sorry," I replied, afraid that I had accidentally released an unpleasant odor. Then I realized Chris was talking about the situation with Tim.

"It sure does," said Larrabe, coming up to join us.

"What kind of a kid would betray another kid like that, anyway?"

This was reassuring. Clearly Larrabe thought of me as one of the class, rather than as "The Purple Outsider."

Before long a circle of kids had gathered around me, all telling me how sorry they were about what had happened. It was as if they feared that they shared the guilt, or had somehow been part of it. I felt a glow as I basked in the warmth of their acceptance. Finally I felt as if I belonged here!

The strange thing was, I was not actually that upset about the picture. The ban on publicity about my life in school comes from the Fatherly One, who wants me to have "a normal experience" in my education. (Why he thinks I can have a normal experience when I am the only kid on the planet with purple skin and a knob growing out of his head is more than I can explain. But if I have learned anything from living on four different planets, it's that no matter where you go, adults have weird ideas.)

What I *was* upset about was that my friend—my *supposed* friend—had taken advantage of me in this way. I felt an ache in my *clinkus,* the sickening pang that comes from the sorrow of betrayal.

This ache, of course, made me all the more willing to accept the sympathy of the other kids. To my astonishment, even Jordan seemed to relax in his attitude toward me. "I always knew Tompkins was a jerk," he said smugly. "Nice to have my instincts confirmed."

Though most of the kids came to speak to me during this break, Linnsy did not. She simply sat on the window ledge, looking troubled and unhappy. I wanted to ask her what she was thinking about, but it was not easy to get away from the group of kids surrounding me.

Besides, I was enjoying their attention.

Tim had still not returned by recess time. My fear that I would be alone on the playground proved to be unfounded as, once again, several kids gathered around me.

It was interesting to observe that when Jordan walked up, most of them pulled back a little, as if acknowledging his right to move to the head of the group.

"So, did you get a little taste of reality this morning, Pleskit?" he asked. His tone was aggressive, but not as nasty as it sometimes is.

McNally was standing close by. I could tell he was ready to move fast if necessary.

"I'm not sure I understand," I replied.

Jordan rolled his eyes. "Wake up and smell the Starbucks, Plesk-o. It's not *you* Tim likes. It's your purple-osity. He was making friends with an alien, not a person."

I did not like this idea, partly because the thought had crossed my own mind more than once. To push it aside, I brought up another issue. "I'm not concerned about Tim right now," I said, not entirely truthfully. "What I really want to know is why *you* dislike me so much."

Jordan laughed. "I don't dislike you. I act that way toward everyone! It's just part of my 'tude. You know—part of being cool."

That word again. This idea of being "cool" is one of the most perplexing things about Earthlings.

Jordan draped his arm over my shoulder.

McNally started forward.

"Chill, Secret Agent Man," said Jordan. "I'm not gonna hurt your boy. I've decided to make him my pal."

McNally's face was expressionless. Brad Kent, however, looked worried. I could see he was afraid I was going to take his place as Jordan's second-in-command and chief butt-kisser. I could have told him this was not a job I particularly desired, but this was not the moment for it.

From the moment Jordan said he was going to be my pal, I could feel my place in the social structure of sixth grade begin to change.

I mention this mostly to try to give some excuse for the things that happened afterward. Despite my friendship with Tim—which was now very much in question, of course—I had been feeling like a total outsider. I wanted to be accepted, to be part of things, maybe even to be "cool." So I ignored my internal warning systems and let myself relax into the idea that Jordan could be my friend.

The Fatherly One has told me that one of the most important tools you can have in the adult world is charm—the ability to make people like you and want to be with you. Jordan's behavior is often disgusting. Even so, he has this charm, and plenty of it. When he turned it on that day, it was like sudden sunshine after a week of rain.

At last I understood why Jordan had the standing he did in the class, understood why the others wanted to be near him and accepted him as their leader.

This charm thing is a great and dangerous gift.

I hardly noticed when Tim came onto the playground.

I was too busy talking with Jordan.

CHAPTER 9

[TIM]

A TERRIFYING DEVELOPMENT

(FROM THE JOURNAL OF TIM TOMPKINS)

The good news was, the security guys couldn't pin anything on me. Despite the cold terror that gripped my gut when they pulled me out of class, this didn't really surprise me, since there was nothing *to* pin on me. I had never seen that camera before in my life. They questioned me six ways from Sunday, but finally had to let me go. Even then I don't think they believed the camera wasn't mine. They just couldn't prove that it *was*—especially since it didn't have any of my fingerprints on it.

When I got back to the room, everyone was outside.

Missing—One Brain!

I hurried outside, too, eager to talk to Pleskit so that I could explain the mix-up.

I also wanted to start a little snooping of my own, to see if I could figure out who had stashed that camera in my desk. I can't figure out if someone was trying to frame me, or if it was just an accident. I have three theories about how that camera got there.

Here they are, in increasing order of badness:

(1) Someone came to school with a camera for some other reason and panicked when they realized there was going to be a problem about the picture in the paper. This unknown person shoved the camera in my desk just so he or she wouldn't get caught with it, even though he or she hadn't actually done anything wrong.

(2) The camera really did belong to the sneak photographer, who had ditched it in my desk for basically the same reason.

(3) The camera had been planted by someone who wanted to get me in trouble.

The last theory is the really scary one. Who would be trying to get me in trouble? And why?

The obvious candidate, of course, is Jordan. But this doesn't really seem like his style.

I have to think about this.

Meanwhile, back to what happened after my "interview" with the agents.

When I went out onto the playground, I was horrified to see Jordan putting his arm around Pleskit's shoulders and doing his patented buddy-buddy act. Even though Jordan is the biggest pain my own personal butt has ever suffered from, I know that when he decides to turn on the charm, no one can resist.

Despite the fact that I basically hate him, I'd like to figure him out. He is one weird ball of wax.

"Hey, Pleskit," I said, trying to sound cool and casual. "Going over to the Dark Side?"

He looked at me like he didn't know me and said, "I am trying to get another perspective on things, Tim. Perhaps we can discuss it later."

Then he walked off with Jordan.

I couldn't believe it! I was the only kid in class who had been totally accepting of Pleskit from the moment he got here, and now he was stiffing me for the one kid who had been most *un*accepting of him. I tried to tell myself it was a bad dream, but the snickers I heard around me were all too real.

"If they gave a merit badge for friend-snatching, that Jordan kid could get it without raising a sweat," said a voice beside me.

I looked to my right, then looked down. The new kid, Larrabe, was standing there. (He really *is* short!)

"Wanna come to my house after school?" he said. "I can show you my collection of matchbooks from famous restaurants."

"Thanks, Larrabe," I answered. "But I don't really feel like it."

"Okay," he said. "That's cool." But his shoulders slumped as he walked away.

I felt like a total creep. I had just given Larrabe the kind of brush-off I have experienced in my own life far too many times. But I had been telling the truth. I really didn't feel like it. I was too upset about what was going on with Pleskit—not to mention the fact that at the moment everyone still thought *I* was the one who had taken that photo for the newspaper.

Well, not everyone. I was still looking at Larrabe, wondering if I should go after him and say something when Brianna, the other new kid, came up to me.

"What was it like to talk to all those guards?" she asked breathlessly.

"Oh, not so bad," I said. I was trying to sound casual, but I was having a hard time because I had suddenly gotten distracted by her smell, which was kind of warm and flowery. This is something that had never happened to me with a girl before, and it startled me. I blinked and shook my head.

"Tim?" she asked.

I shook my head again. "Sorry. I think I was having a flashback or something. It was a very upsetting experience."

"So how did it turn out?" she asked, looking worried.

I shrugged. "They got upset because I wouldn't admit to anything. But since the camera wasn't mine, there was nothing to admit. Finally they had to let me go."

She smiled in relief. "I figured if they let you come back, it must not have been yours. I didn't think it was anyway."

"They tried to bully me into confessing that it was," I continued, which was actually kind of true. They hadn't hit me or anything. But, psychologically speaking, they had been pretty rough.

"That's awful!" she cried, her eyes getting wide.

"I got through it," I said, shrugging modestly, the way Lance Driscoll always used to on "Tarbox Moon Warriors."

Brianna smiled, which was sort of like unleashing a sunbeam. "You must be pretty cool," she said. Then she put her fingers to her mouth and rolled her eyes a little, as if she had said too much. "Well, see you later."

She turned and walked away, leaving me feeling slightly dizzy, and wishing that I could still smell her.

* * *

I didn't have a chance to see Pleskit after school, since he had to leave early because his Fatherly One was taking him to a party being thrown by some king or other.

I did, however, have a chance to talk to McNally for a minute.

"*You* don't think that camera was mine, do you?" I asked him.

He shook his head. "Nah. Looked like a setup to me. Those morons who questioned you probably knew that, but they had to look like they were doing something, and that was easier than really working."

Obviously he was still bitter about the extra security guys.

"So Pleskit knows it wasn't me, too?" I asked hopefully.

"I'm not sure," said McNally, sounding a little troubled. "Hard to say what Captain Weasel has been doing to his brain this afternoon."

By "Captain Weasel" I understood him to mean Jordan.

"It's too bad our plan to shrink Captain Weasel didn't work," I said wistfully.

McNally stiffened, and I could tell I was in dicey territory. He was still unhappy about the fact that Pleskit and I had roped him into helping us with our disastrous attempt to shrink Jordan.

"Tell you what, Tim," he said coldly. "Next time someone—say, a special agent—suggests a code name so you can discuss a given person in public, flash back to this little tip: Don't immediately use that code name in a sentence that would let anyone listening in instantly know exactly who the code name refers to!"

He turned and stalked away.

Great. I had just screwed up my last link to Pleskit.

I stood there for a minute, feeling like I had just had the air sucked out of my lungs. Then Brianna walked up. "Man, he looked angry," she said, sounding awed.

"Yeah, he kinda is."

Then—and this was the worst and scariest part of this whole terrible day—I did something I've never done before. I don't know why I did it. Maybe because I was so upset about everything—the guards, the camera, Pleskit, Jordan, McNally, the whole rotten mess. Maybe just because something is happening in my brain that I don't understand. Maybe just because of that amazing smell, which I had not been able to get out of my mind all afternoon.

Anyway, I'm not sure why, but I turned to Brianna and said, "Can I walk you home?"

"Oh, Tim, I'm sorry, I can't today. But maybe sometime soon. I think I'd like that!"

Then she smiled and walked away.

Now, here's the horrifying part: That was four hours ago, and I haven't been able to stop thinking about it since.

Just when I thought life couldn't get any worse, the unthinkable has happened.

I'm in love!

I could just puke.

CHAPTER 10

[PLESKIT] SQUAMBUL

The next day another big headline screamed from the front of *The National News:*

CLOUD OF SECRECY DESCENDS OVER SCHOOL

There was no photo of me this time. There was, however, a subheading, also in big letters:

"Innocent Boy Terrorized by Security Guards"

Next to it was a picture of Tim.

The paper was all over the school, of course. Some of the kids were slightly amused. Most of the adults were cranky. And *everyone* seemed to think that Tim was the source, which was no surprise, given the fact that the story was so sympathetic to him.

"Looks like I assigned the code name 'Captain Weasel' to the wrong kid," muttered McNally when he saw the paper.

I looked at him in puzzlement. "I beg your pardon?"

"Nothing," he said. "Forget it."

But how could I forget it? The person who had most befriended me on my arrival seemed to have turned out to have a hidden side of sneakiness that I had not suspected.

This was very disturbing. "Sneaky" is different from "tricky." People who are tricky have a certain set of rules for themselves, and they work within those rules. "Sneaky" does not imply the same code of ethics. Tricky people fool you honorably, right in front of your face. Sneaky people do it behind your back. The Fatherly One has high regard for those who are tricky, but no respect at all for those who are merely sneaky.

I was so disturbed by all this that I could not bring myself to talk to Tim that day. This did not mean I was alone or lonely. The class seemed to be getting more comfortable with me. And Jordan was still acting extremely friendly, which I was enjoying.

"You know what you really need to do, Pleskit?"

he said, when we were sitting at lunch that day.

"Achieve good grades, excel in all subjects, avoid trouble, and make the Fatherly One proud?"

Jordan snorted. "On your planet, maybe. No, what you need to do is bring something extremely cool to school."

"This will not be easy, mostly because I still do not entirely understand this concept of 'cool.'"

I flattened the *squambul* pod I had brought for lunch. It released a sharp aroma.

"Whoo!" said Jordan, waving a hand in front of his face. "That is one nasty-smelling lunch, Plesk-o."

"*Squambul* is considered a great delicacy on many planets," I said, spreading the purple-and-green contents of the pod on the palm of my hand.

Jordan sighed, and I could tell he was trying to be patient. "Bring in something no one around here has ever seen before—and not something to shrink *me* with!" he added, referring to the unfortunate events of the previous week.

"I have already apologized for that error in judgment."

"Well, you still owe me a favor for it."

"But I did not shrink *you,*" I pointed out. "I shrank Tim and Ms. Weintraub."

"Yeah, but that was only because you screwed up. I was the one you *planned* to shrink."

In this, Jordan had a point. It was a point that he continued to make over the next several days. He was very good at this, very persuasive. When I mentioned this to McNally he said, "Doesn't surprise me. Jordan will probably be a lawyer when he grows up. Or maybe a used car salesman."

Three days went by without another article in *The National News*. Then true disaster struck. The cover of *The National Scoop* (the "skeezy" supermarket paper) featured a full-page photograph of me licking *squambul* off my palm. Jordan's face was also visible, twisted in an expression of horror. The headline read:

ALIEN BOYS BIZARRE EATING HABITS DISGUST CLASSMATES!

Ms. Weintraub used the occasion for a quick lesson on how to use apostrophes, and pointed out that we shouldn't necessarily trust a paper that can't even punctuate its headlines correctly.

Tim was hauled away for questioning again. To our surprise, so was every other member of the class—

SCOOP INVESTIGATION
CITY WORK CREWS DISCOVER THAT ALIEN EMBASSEY ACTUALLY WORLD'S
LARGEST
BUG ZAPPER!!!
RADIATION BURNS? FACT OR FICTION
DOES IT ATTRACT AIRPLANES?
DO TAXPAYERS PAY ELECTRICITY BILL?
STARTLING CONFESSION!
FROM MONSTER MOON-MAN BEHIND THE MASK OF...
"MY TEACHER IS AN ALIEN!"
THE NATIONAL
SCOOP
RLD
LUSIVE
WS
EVEN BIGFOOT FELT ILL AFTER SEEING OUR SICK PICS!
ALIEN
BOYS
BIZARRE
EATING HABITS
DISGUST
CLASSMATES!

except for Jordan, since it was pretty clear he had not taken the photograph.

No one was happy. Even worse, some of my classmates seemed to blame me for their being questioned, which struck me as being especially unfair.

When I got back to the embassy that afternoon, I went to consult with the Grandfatherly One. It was not an entirely satisfactory conversation, as he spent most of the time I was with him complaining about being bored.

"I've got to get out into the world, Pleskit," he said. "My circuits are shriveling!"

That evening the Fatherly One convened an embassy-wide meeting to discuss the situation.

Of course, since Earth is a scarcely civilized and relatively unimportant planet, we are a small and understaffed embassy. Therefore, such a meeting does not include all that many beings. In this case it was me, the Fatherly One, Barvgis, Shhh-foop, McNally, and the Butt.

(Normally Shhh-foop would not be asked to a staff meeting, but the Fatherly One wanted everyone present for this one. Yet when I suggested we should include the Grandfatherly One, the Fatherly One vetoed the idea. This caused me to suspect/fear that the Fatherly One and the Grandfatherly One had had a conflict of some sort.)

We met in the small conference room, seated around a table made of blue shiftstone from the Planet Arbingle. The table is one of the Fatherly One's proudest possessions, since Arbingle's shiftstone is known across the galaxy for the beauty of its swirling patterns, which change slowly but steadily, so that the table's surface is never the same from one hour to the next.

"Can you explain to me, Ms. Buttsman," said the Fatherly One, "why the Earth media are doing this to Pleskit?"

"Because they are run by bloodsucking corporate entities that will do anything to make a dollar," said Ms. Buttsman.

The Fatherly One looked puzzled. "That is generally true of successful companies across the galaxy. In fact, in most cases it is considered admirable. However, in all cases that we are aware of this behavior is reserved for adult beings. Young people are shielded from it. Does your culture have no respect for the tenderness of youth, and the need to protect childlings from such things while they are still growing?"

McNally laughed out loud. Everyone turned to look at him. "Excuse me," he said. "But the short answer to your question is: No."

"Ah," said the Fatherly One. "I see. Well, your culture is clearly even more troubled than I had realized. Now, since we cannot count on the culture to stop this intrusion on Pleskit's privacy, we will have to handle it ourselves. Ms. Buttsman, are there any pressures we can bring to bear against this news company to get them to desist in their efforts to report on Pleskit's life in school?"

Ms. Buttsman pursed her lips, then said, "Not many. We could appeal to their decency, but as they have none, it is unlikely that would do us any good. For the most part, their behavior is protected by our laws granting freedom of the press."

The Fatherly One belched in disgust. "We have similar laws, but they do not apply to youngsters. What a culture! Mr. McNally—I am going to ask you to apply your best efforts to discovering the source of this information."

"I will do my best, Meenom," said McNally. "However, my primary concern must remain Pleskit's physical safety."

An unpleasant smell drifted from the *sphen-gnutksher* of the Fatherly One.

Suddenly I had what Tim calls a "brainstorm." It seemed like a brilliant idea, a way to solve three problems at once.

CHAPTER 11

[TIM]

ADVICE (STILL FROM THE JOURNAL OF TIM TOMPKINS)

The days since the newspaper articles started have been very painful. I had been dreaming about meeting an alien all my life. Then, when I did, we had actually become friends. It was the best thing that ever happened to me.

And now it's over.

This afternoon I finally decided to ask Linnsy for her advice. She has this amazing ability to move between social groups, so she can talk to the popular kids and the sports kids and the nerdy kids, and they all seem to like her. It's like being able to swim with the fishes *and* fly with the birds.

(Sometimes I wonder if Linnsy is an alien, too.)

Anyway, I asked if I could walk home with her after school today, and she said yes—which was unusual in itself, since she mostly doesn't walk with me anymore.

Actually, what she said was "Wouldn't you rather be walking home with Brianna?"

Well, the answer to that was yes. But I hadn't been able to pull a walk with Brianna off yet, mostly because she was usually busy with dance lessons or something. However, I was also smart enough to know that this was not a case that called for absolute honesty. So I just said, "Come on, Linns—for old times' sake."

She rolled her eyes. "You're such a doof, Tim. But yeah, I'll walk home with you."

We didn't talk much most of the way. But when we got to the bridge, we stopped so we could look at the embassy. That was when I told her about what was bothering me. Well, I told her about how upset I was over the Pleskit situation. I didn't talk about Brianna. I wasn't ready to say anything like *that* out loud.

"I was wondering when you were going to ask me about Pleskit," she said.

"You were?" I asked in astonishment.

Linnsy rolled her eyes. "Why do you think I agreed to walk home with you? I figured unless I gave you a chance, you were never going to open your mouth."

I wasn't sure whether to be insulted, angry, or grateful. This happens a lot when I talk to Linnsy.

I decided to just go for the info.

"So what should I do?" I asked. "My best friend is hanging around with my worst enemy because he thinks I've been passing information about him to the newspapers."

"Well, the first question is: Have you?"

"Linnsy!"

She shook her head. "Nice try, Tim. But shock and outrage do not constitute an answer. In fact, they're as apt to mean you're guilty as not guilty. I use that tactic on my mother all the time when I want to avoid a question. But don't try it on me. I'm too smart for it."

This was even more outrageous as far as I was concerned. But then I remembered that I had also used this tactic on my own mother a couple of times, so I decided not to get too offended.

"Okay, the straight answer is: No. Absolutely, positively not. It never occurred to me. Even if it had occurred to me, I wouldn't have done it. In fact, we had reporters calling the house before this started, and Mom and I told them to go bite blue monkeys—even when they offered us big bucks."

"Okay, that's what I figured. I just wanted to be sure."

"Well, it wasn't me."

"I believe you, Tim. I just had to check."

"All right," I said, still feeling huffy. "I just wanted to get that clear."

"Good. Now go do the same thing for Pleskit."

"Do what?"

"Get things clear with him. Talk to him. Tell him what you just told me."

This was good advice.

I did not follow it.

Why?

This is hard to explain, since I'm not entirely sure I understand it myself. I guess it had to do with pride. I was hurt that Pleskit had believed the worst of me without more proof. I wanted *him* to come to me.

There's a word for people who wait around for their friends to make the first move to patch things up after they've had a quarrel.

The word is "lonely."

CHAPTER 12

[PLESKIT]
MY BRAINSTORM

Jordan had been hounding me to bring some-thing "cool" to school.

The Grandfatherly One had been pleading with me to get him out of the embassy so he could experience Earthly culture.

The Fatherly One felt we had to take matters regarding the discovery of the leak to the newspapers into our own hands.

And I had a plan that would solve all three of these issues at once: I would take the Grandfatherly One to school with me!

The first question was whether I would clear this with

the Fatherly One before doing it. I decided to discuss that matter with the being who would be most affected by the decision—namely, the Grandfatherly One.

He was not in a good mood when I entered his chamber. "Ah, come to pay your last respects to a once venerated ancestor who is soon to leave this world?" he muttered.

"How can you leave this world?" I asked.

"By dying!"

"But you already did that!" I cried in alarm.

"Hah! That was mere death of the body. I am facing a far more serious challenge now, Pleskit. I am about to die the ultimate death, the death of the mind, a death brought on by . . . *boredom*!" He paused to let that sink in, then said, "So, what did you come to talk about?"

He seemed ripe for my idea. Still, I knew I had to approach this carefully. So I said, "I have some problems at school that I would like to discuss. Perhaps they will help relieve your boredom."

"Oy! Your Fatherly One used to consult me on matters of interplanetary importance. Now I am to resolve schoolyard disputes."

"Oy?"

"It's sort of an all-purpose expression of despair. One of the most useful Earthling words I have discovered so far."

The Grandfatherly One is much better at absorbing new languages than I am—partly because he has little else to do while sitting in his vat.

"However," he continued, "I'm certain you didn't come here to discuss language. What's your problem at school?"

"Two problems, actually," I said. Then I filled him in on both the way Jordan was bugging me to bring something "cool" to school and the matter of the leaked news stories.

"Sounds like *three* problems to me," he said, "given that you've had a rift with your previous companion. Do you really think Tim is the one who has been ratting on you? He didn't seem like the type."

"All evidence points in his direction."

"Evidence is useful. However, since one almost never has *all* the evidence, it is easy to be misled by it. I repeat: Your friend Tim did not strike me as the type to do such a thing."

"I don't know," I said uneasily. "I sometimes fear

that the only reason he befriended me to begin with is that he is so interested in aliens."

"So he should make friends with someone who bores him?"

I emitted the tangy smell of frustration, something I am often driven to do when talking with the Grandfatherly One. "If someone is going to be my friend, I want them to like me because I am me, not just because I am from another planet!"

"Liking has to start somewhere. Do you think this Jordan kid likes you because you are *you*?"

The voice of the Grandfatherly One was deeply skeptical.

"I do not know," I replied. "When he is being nice to one, it is like a flood of sunshine."

"And when he's not, it's like a bath of cold mud. I know the type. I've already told you he's dangerous. Now, listen, Pleskit, I think I've got the answer to both our problems."

"You do?" I asked eagerly.

"Yes. I think you should take me to school. I'll at least get out of this place, and you'll have the benefit of my insight and advice. Also, maybe I can pick up some clues that you've missed about who's dropping info to the newsies. Plus, I like to believe that I would qualify as 'cool,' which should shut up this Jordan creature for a while."

This, of course, was exactly what I had been hoping the Grandfatherly One would suggest. However, I did not want to seem too eager.

"Are you sure that's a good idea?" I asked doubtfully.

"Do I have any other kind?" he replied indignantly.

"All right—let's do it!"

"Oh, and Pleskit—"

"Yes, O Venerated One?"

"No need to tell your parental unit about this, if you know what I mean."

"I believe I understand, Grandfatherly One."

"And one more thing, Pleskit."

"Yes?"

"Next time you have an idea like this, why not just tell me about it instead of working so hard to get me to suggest it myself? It'll be easier on both of us."

"You are wise beyond your years, Grandfatherly One."

"Yeah, yeah, yeah. That's why Meenom kept me

around. For all the good it's done. See you tomorrow, kid."

I belched respectfully and left the room.

The next morning I returned to the chamber of the Grandfatherly One. Using a special mechanism attached to the side of his vat, I transferred him to the Brain Transport Device, a portable unit used for traveling. This BTD is about the size of what Earthlings call a "boombox." Its central section is filled with the same electrolyte solution that is in the main tank. Attached to the sides are smaller versions of the visual, auditory, and scent-receiving devices, as well as a speaker tube. The primary limitation on the container is that, because of its size, it can only support life for about twelve hours. So I had to be sure to bring the brain back each night after school.

Once I had the Grandfatherly One inside the BTD, he said, "I'm going to activate the shutdown mode now, Pleskit."

"What for?"

"Because, O-beloved-but-not-entirely-thinking-straight-second-generation-offspring, it will be easier for us to get past that horrible Buttsman woman if she doesn't realize that you are removing a highly valuable artifact—namely, my brain—from the embassy."

"Ah," I said. "You are correct as usual, Grandfatherly One."

"Skip the flattery. Just get me out of here."

And with that he activated the shutdown mode. The sides of the BTD darkened. The tubular extensions retracted. In less than a moment it looked like nothing more than a bright purple box with shiny sides.

The Grandfatherly One had been wise in his precautions. As I left for school that morning, the dreaded Ms. Buttsman said, "What do you have in the case, Pleskit?"

"Something for show-and-tell," I said, remembering a classroom ritual that Tim had described to me.

"I'm glad to see you approaching your studies in the proper spirit," she said primly.

I left the embassy with high hopes. I thought this was a brilliant idea.

The Grandfatherly One, who is wise and experienced, agreed.

Given all that, how was I to know that I had just embarked on one of the biggest mistakes of my life?

CHAPTER 13

[TIM]
THE PERILS OF LOVE

Pleskit walked into the classroom with a strange-looking purple box. He set it on his desk, knocked on the top, and said, "We're here, you can come out now."

I couldn't tell whether the sides of the box rolled up, slid in, or simply changed so that they were clear. However it happened, the dark purple vanished so that you could look directly into the container to see . . . the brain of the Grandfatherly One! Several snaky tubes extended from the box. I recognized them at once; they were small versions of the sensors the Grandfatherly One uses to pick up sights, sounds, and smells.

I felt another painful surge of jealousy, the worst one yet. A few days ago I would have been in on bringing the Grandfatherly One to class. Now all I could do was stand at the edge of things and watch while the other kids clustered around Pleskit's desk.

"What's that?" asked Jordan. "Your lunch?"

"I'll thank you to keep a civil tongue in your head, young man!" snapped the Grandfatherly One.

Jordan jumped back. "Whoa! It talks!"

"I not only talk, I *think*—which is not something that can be said of everyone who can form words. I have opinions, fascinating anecdotes, and a wealth of information."

Jordan's eyes were getting wider. McNally looked amused. Ms. Weintraub stepped forward. "Would you care to introduce your . . . uh . . . your *guest*, Pleskit?"

"Certainly," said Pleskit. "This is the brain of Ven-traah Komquist, Fatherly One to my own Fatherly One, which makes him my Grandfatherly One."

"Not much left of him," said Jordan with a smirk.

"Just the good part," said the Grandfatherly One. "What are they going to save when you go, Slick? Your hairdo?"

McNally laughed out loud. Jordan looked really angry but didn't say anything.

Brianna had been staring at the brain in total fascination. Taking a step closer, she said, "I suppose you can tell us a lot about your world, sir."

"Sure can," said the Grandfatherly One. "And

there's a lot I'd like to set straight about it, given some of the stuff that's been showing up in your newspapers. But I can tell you more than that, kid. I've lived on dozens of worlds. Had fascinating adventures, hairbreadth escapes, heart-stopping romances. For example, there was the time I was lost in the swamps of Mingbat Seven—that is, the seventh star out from the planet Mingbat—and was nearly devoured by a demented *wungborkle.*"

"A *wungborkle?*" asked Larrabe.

"Hmmm," said the Grandfatherly One. "I guess you'd consider it sort of an intelligent snake—except this *wungborkle* had four hands and was about thirty feet long."

It was a great story, and the class listened in absolute fascination. After a while Ms. Weintraub decided to cancel her plans for the morning and just let us talk to the Grandfatherly One. She moved his box—which Pleskit told us was a "Brain Transport Device"—to a stool in the corner. Then we all sat in a circle to listen to his stories.

After a couple of hours Ms. Weintraub said, "We have to take a little break now, sir—it's time for recess. Would you like to go outside with us?"

"Nah, I think I'll just go into shutdown mode for a bit. I'm not used to talking this much—haven't had an audience in quite a while. Just leave me in here. We can pick up where we left off when you come back."

Before Ms. Weintraub could answer, the Grandfatherly One's sensory extensions slithered into the side panels. The speaker stem pulled in. The clear sides grew dark, completely hiding the brain. In little more than an instant, the BTD looked like a plain purple box. Or maybe I should say a "mysterious" purple box, since it didn't look quite like anything I had ever seen before.

"Will the Grandfatherly One be all right if I leave him here?" Pleskit asked McNally.

"Should be fine," replied McNally bitterly. "If we had any more security at this school, even you couldn't get in!"

As we lined up to go outside, I glanced around, trying to spot Brianna. I was hoping I could walk beside her.

She was nowhere to be seen.

I felt a ripple of fear. Was she all right? Had anything happened to her?

I told Ms. Weintraub I needed to go to the bathroom, which was at least partially true. But what I really wanted to do was look for Brianna.

Maybe she was having a hard time adjusting to the new school. Maybe she just needed someone friendly to talk to—someone who could help her feel better. Maybe *I* could be that someone!

I went to the bathroom, which technically meant I hadn't been lying. Then I wandered up and down the halls, hoping to catch a glimpse of her. I passed three or four security guards who looked at me suspiciously. But no Brianna.

Finally I gave up and decided I had better get outside before someone nailed me and gave me detention. But as I came around the corner toward our room, I saw Brianna standing just outside our classroom door. She glanced around, then slipped back into the room.

What was going on?

I hurried toward the room to see if she was all right.

Before I could get there, the alarm bell rang.

Most of the rooms in our hall were already empty, since it was the sixth-grade recess time. But there were a couple of fifth-grade rooms at the end of the hall, and those kids came pouring out of their doors.

I should have just joined them and left the building. But I had noticed that Brianna had not come back out of our room. So I slipped into Mrs. Konkel's room, two doors up from ours, and waited till the hall was clear again.

Then I headed back to our room to find out what was up with Brianna.

Love does strange things to a guy.

Also, it can get you in a lot of trouble.

CHAPTER 14

[PLESKIT] TERROR!

Until the alarm bell rang, I had been having a good time at recess. We had only been outside a few minutes when Jordan approached me and said, "Hey, Pleskit—your grandfather's brain is totally cool. Why didn't you bring him to school before this?"

"Yeah," said Brad. "What were you doing—holdin' out on us?"

"I did not realize you would find the brain of an elderly alien being so fascinating," I said, feeling somewhat surprised.

Jordan looked a little startled. Then he smirked

and said, "He's not just a brain, man; he's an interplanetary adventurer!"

I decided not to mention that the Grandfatherly One's stories are not always entirely reliable.

We were joined by several other kids, all of them excited about having met the Grandfatherly One. Suddenly our talk was interrupted by a horrible blaring sound. The doors of the school burst open. Students and teachers came pouring out of the building.

Ms. Weintraub raised her hand and shouted for us to join her. Most of us kids hurried to her side. I noticed, however, that Jordan ambled over as if it was no big deal.

Some kids started to talk, but Ms. Weintraub shushed us to silence. Larrabe, who was standing next to me, whispered, "Don't worry, Pleskit—it's just a fire drill. Standard operating procedure. No big deal."

A moment later one of the teachers came over to Ms. Weintraub and whispered something to her.

Ms. Weintraub's eyes grew wide, and she looked distraught.

I desperately wanted to know what the other teacher had said. However, I knew Ms. Weintraub would not tell me. This was one of those adult things.

McNally had no problem with asking. Taking Ms. Weintraub's arm, he said, "What is it? What's going on?"

Before she could answer, Mr. Philgrinn, the gym teacher, came running over. "Get the class back!" he cried. "Get back!"

"Why?" asked McNally.

"There's a bomb in the building!"

McNally's eyes flashed. But he kept his voice calm as he said, "You mean someone called in a bomb threat."

"No!" cried Mr. Philgrinn. "It's a real bomb! The security guards actually found it!"

It was my turn to get upset. "The Grandfatherly One is still inside!" I cried. I started toward the building. "I can't let him be blown up!"

"You're not going anywhere," said McNally, grabbing me by the arm. Ms. Weintraub grabbed my other arm. As soon as she did, McNally let go.

"Hold on to him," he said, starting forward himself.

"Where do you think you're going, McNally?" cried Ms. Weintraub.

"To get the Grandfatherly One!"

"You can't go back in there!" she shouted. She let

go of my arm and lunged forward to grab his. "The building has been evacuated."

I darted forward again. Ms. Weintraub let go of McNally, and they both grabbed me.

"You hold him," said McNally. "I'm going for the Grandfatherly One. No one else knows he's there. I've got to get him out."

Ms. Weintraub started to speak, then just nodded.

McNally raced toward the building, flung open the door, disappeared inside.

A deep silence fell over the class.

We stared at the school in horror, waiting. . . .

CHAPTER 15

[TIM]

THE BRAIN-NAPPER

It was weird to be in the building when everyone else had left. Part of my brain was screaming that I should get out, too. Unfortunately, another part, less intelligent but more powerful, was insisting I find out what was going on with Brianna. So instead of bolting for the outside doors, I glanced around, then hurried across the hall. Dropping to the floor, I crawled to the door. (The reason I did this is that I figured someone is less apt to see you peeking around a corner if you're at floor level. Also, my sneakers tend to be slightly squeaky.)

I looked into the room.

Missing—One Brain!

Brianna was standing beside Pleskit's desk.

Two things startled me.

First, the Grandfatherly One's BTD was no longer sitting on Pleskit's desk. What had happened to it? Had Pleskit put the BTD under the desk for safekeeping? I didn't remember him doing that.

The second thing that startled me was Brianna. Her voice soft but intense. She was swearing. I mean *really* swearing—the kind of words you can get thrown out of school for. I could feel my eyes getting wider. Who would have guessed my sweet Brianna could talk like that?

After a minute she pulled a tiny recorder from her pocket and began muttering into it.

That was when I *finally* started to get suspicious about her.

Suddenly she turned and headed for the door. I slid back and pressed myself against the wall, hoping (a) she hadn't already seen me and (b) she would turn in the other direction.

Luck was with me.

Before I could feel much of a sense of relief, I heard a sound to my right. Someone else was coming! I scooted through the door and into the room. Where to hide?

The best spot was obvious—under Ms. Weintraub's desk.

It was only when I got under there that I realized it wouldn't be such a good idea if the person coming into the room was Ms. Weintraub herself.

Footsteps. Then a familiar voice—not Ms. Weintraub, but McNally. Pressing my face to the floor, I could see his feet from under the front of the desk. (Seeing from under Ms. Weintraub's desk had been a lot easier a couple of weeks earlier, when I was only two inches tall.)

He was standing by Pleskit's desk. And he was cursing, just like Brianna had.

What the heck was going on here?

McNally stomped around the room for a moment, then left.

I slipped out from under the desk, not sure whether I should follow McNally, go after Brianna, or just get out of the school—which is what I should have done in the first place.

I decided to go after Brianna. (If this is the kind of stupid thing that love makes you do, I hope I don't fall in love again for a long, long time.) I wasn't sure I could find her: The delay while I hid from McNally had given her a couple of minutes' lead time, and she could have been anywhere in the school by now. After a moment of dithering, I just went in the direction I had last seen her, hoping I would spot her.

When I reached the corner, I dropped to the floor again and peered around the edge. Brianna was at the end of the hall, doing the same thing! Well, she was still on her feet. But she had pressed herself tight to the wall and was looking around the next corner.

A second later she scooted around it.

I set off after her. Trying to be both silent and fast, I cursed when I heard my sneakers squeak. I hoped she hadn't heard them, too!

When I got to the next corner I made the same spy-type movement.

Brianna was about halfway down the hall. As I watched, she slipped into the art room. This was directly across the hall from Ms. Zammit's music room, which was the room that had been taken over by the security guards.

I stayed pressed against the wall, trying to decide what to do next. Before I could make up my mind, I heard a lot of yelling and shouting from the security room. Suddenly a whole group of guards came bursting out of the room. From what I could make out, they were heading for Mr. Grand's office. (Fortunately, this was in the opposite direction from where I was lurking.)

As soon as they were gone, Brianna slipped out of her hiding place and scooted across the hall, into the security room.

I scurried down the hall to see what she was up to. I stopped just outside the door, then dropped again and peered around the edge.

The Grandfatherly One's BTD was sitting on a table.

Brianna glanced around, then picked it up.

I should have said something. I should have shouted for help. But I still couldn't believe my sweet Brianna was really up to anything bad. (All right, you can stop gagging. I told you: Love has *serious* side effects on a person's brain.)

Besides, even if she was doing something bad, I didn't want to get her in trouble. Maybe I could save her from herself. Or if she did get in trouble, I imagined myself standing beside her, taking some of the flak for her. I had an image of her being so grateful that she threw her arms around my neck and . . . well, never mind. Let's just say that at the moment I was not entirely in my right mind.

Missing—One Brain!

So when Brianna headed for the door with the Grandfatherly One's brain, I scooted across the hall and into the very room where she herself had been hiding just a few seconds earlier. Pressing myself against the wall, I listened for her footsteps. Would she walk past me, or in the other direction?

Past me.

I slipped out of the room and started to follow, wondering as I did where she was planning to go that she wouldn't be seen by other people.

It didn't take long before I had my answer.

Hanging a sharp right, she walked straight into the one place in the school I had never been.

The girls' room!

CHAPTER 16

[PLESKIT]
MISSING PERSONS

When McNally came racing back out onto the playground, he did not look heroic. Mostly he looked upset.

Actually, "terrified" would be a better word.

As soon as he spoke, I shared his condition.

"The Grandfatherly One is missing!" he gasped.

Cold fingers seemed to grip my *clinkus*. "What did you say?"

"Your Grandfatherly One is not there," said McNally. "I have no idea what's happened to him."

It was only by closing my eyes and counting for a moment that I was able to keep from falling into *kleptra*.

Finally I was driven to a moment of interpretive dance, always the best and surest way to dispose of emotions that are too intense to handle.

Waving one hand above my head, I began turning in a slow circle, chanting, "Woo. Wooo-ooo. Wooooaaga, wooooaga, woooo-ah-ah-ah-ah-aga." I took three backward leaps, shook both arms, then kissed my knees. All of this was accompanied by numerous farts and belches, of course, which is a way of expelling not only gas but excess emotions.

Lost in the power of the moment, I did not think about the class. When I was done, I realized they were staring at me in astonishment.

"What a geek!" howled Jordan.

Instantly I felt like a fool. Not so much because Jordan was making fun of me, but because I had been stupid enough to think that he had actually befriended me. I should have known better.

In truth, I *had* known better. But, despite the teachings of the Grandfatherly One, I had been dazzled by Jordan's charm.

Shaken by the revelation of my own foolishness, I turned to look for Tim.

He was not with us.

"Where is Tim?" I cried. "What has happened to him?"

Ms. Weintraub groaned. "If he's still inside the school, I'll kill him!"

"If there's really a bomb in there, you won't need to," pointed out Jordan.

"Hey!" cried Misty Longacres. "Brianna is missing, too!"

"Oo-ooo! Tim and Brianna!" cried several of the girls. Two of them started making kissy noises.

"As if!" said Jordan, his face getting red.

Hardly anyone in the class could believe Tim was capable of actually starting a romance, especially with someone like Brianna. That didn't stop them from giggling about it, though.

The problem was, everyone was ignoring the main issue, namely, that we now had *three* people missing!

I realized this was the main issue at about the same time I realized I was shouting it out loud.

The answer to one-third of my concerns—namely, where was the Grandfatherly One?—arrived more quickly than I expected, when Principal Grand came out of the school to announce that the building had been declared safe to enter.

He looked a little embarrassed.

"False alarm?" asked Ms. Weintraub.

"You could say that," replied Mr. Grand. His voice was sharp and I noticed that I could see more of his teeth than was usual. "The security team was checking your room when they came across Pleskit's Grandfatherly One. The box was so . . . *unusual* . . . that the team thought it was a bomb—which was why we had to evacuate the building."

"Those morons!" cried McNally.

"That was pretty much what Pleskit's Grandfatherly One called them when he woke from his nap." Mr. Grand frowned. "Really, it was very startling when all those . . . *things* came poking out of the box and it began to speak to us." He turned toward me, and I could tell he was forcing himself to be calm when he said, "I must ask you to remember, Pleskit, that all visitors are required to register at the office when they enter the school. Though I was glad to meet Ventraah Komquist—and really, you must explain to me how your family name system works someday—I am also most annoyed that I was not informed we had such a dignitary among us. A little advance knowledge might have saved a lot of trouble!"

Despite Mr. Grand's crankiness, I was enormously relieved. The Grandfatherly One was all right!

I had been concerned about his safety as a venerated ancestor, of course. But I had also been concerned because I had brought him to school without actually gathering the approval of the Fatherly One. If anything had happened to him, I might have found myself in even more trouble than I had been in on Geembol Seven.

Unfortunately, this still did not tell us where Tim and Brianna had gone. But "One crisis at a time," as the Fatherly One is fond of saying.

Leaving Ms. Weintraub to deal with the question of Tim and Brianna, McNally and I went to retrieve the brain of my ancestral unit.

When we entered the room that had been taken over by the security guards, they did not look happy to see us.

"Okay," said McNally. "Give me the brain."

The guards looked at one another nervously. The one who seemed to be their leader cleared his throat. "There's a little problem," he said.

"What problem?" asked McNally.

"We don't have it."

"Well, where is it?"

"We don't know."

"You *what*?" roared McNally. "You boneheads! First you get the entire school terrified over nothing, and now you've lost my client's grandfather? I hope you didn't really want this job, boys, because when this is over I'm going to be using your ID cards for toilet paper. Come on, Pleskit. Let's start looking."

He grabbed me by the arm and pulled me from the room.

"Do you have any idea what could have happened to the Grandfatherly One?" I asked, struggling to keep from either going into *kleptra* or performing another dance.

"Not the vaguest," said McNally through clenched teeth. "But we'd better find him fast, or *I'm* going to be the one kissing his job good-bye."

"This is very upsetting," I said.

"You're not kidding," muttered McNally.

"No, you do not understand. The Grandfatherly One's BTD has a twelve-hour limit on life support. If we do not retrieve him before six o'clock this evening . . ." The fear was too great. At a loss for words, I let my *sphen-gnut-ksher* emit the odor of total despair.

"Oh, man," said McNally, waving his hand in front of his face. "That's the worst one yet, Pleskit!"

"The worst news or the worst smell?"

"Both," said McNally grimly. "Come on, we're heading for the office."

Mr. Grand was standing behind the counter that separates the front of the office from the private rooms in back. He smiled when he saw us. "Well, it's been quite a morning, Mr. McNally. But all's well that ends well, eh?"

"This hasn't ended yet," snarled McNally. "Those idiots sent over to beef up security have *lost* the brain!"

Mr. Grand did the same trick I had seen Tim do on a few occasions, the one where all the color leaves his face and he turns almost pure white.

"What?" he asked, his voice tiny and strangled sounding.

"You heard me," said McNally. "Now, here's what—"

He was interrupted by the telephone. Ms. Blossom, the secretary, picked it up. Her eyes got wide.

Putting her hand over the mouthpiece, she hissed, "It's the embassy."

"What fresh disaster lurches toward us?" I whispered.

Ms. Blossom had taken her hand from the mouthpiece. "Yes, I see. Uh-huh. I see. Well, really, Ms. Buttsman, I'm not sure. . . . Oh, I see. Well, yes. I'll certainly give him the message. Thank you very much."

She put down the phone and stared at it.

"Well, what is it?" cried Mr. Grand.

"The ambassador is on his way to the school."

"What?" shrieked McNally.

"He wants to do a follow-up to last week's assembly. I tried to say that this was a bad time, but Ms. Buttsman said it was the only opening he was likely to have for the next few months."

"Why didn't you tell him the school was closed?" cried Mr. Grand.

"Well, since his son is here right now, I'm not sure he would have believed that," she replied tartly. "Besides, *you're* the one who told him to stop by anytime."

"I say that to all the parents! I don't expect them to actually do it. Now what? Who's going to tell the alien ambassador that we've lost his Fatherly One's brain?" Suddenly his eyes widened and he turned to me. "Pleskit! You understand the interpersonal dynamics of your race better than any of us possibly could. Therefore, I think you should be the one to break this news to your parental unit. Besides, you're the one who brought the brain to school to begin with."

Fresh terror gripped my *clinkus.*

"Start looking!" I cried. "We've got to find that brain!"

CHAPTER 17

[TIM]

REVELATION

The girls' room! Now what was I supposed to do?

For a moment I just stood there, staring at the door like a dog that's been locked out of its house.

"I can't," I whispered.

You must! said a small part of my brain.

"It's forbidden!" I replied, feeling a new terror creep up on me.

It's necessary, insisted my brain.

"But what if I get caught?" I muttered nervously.

What if Brianna escapes because you're afraid? countered my brain.

Whoa! That was a new idea. Was there a window she

could climb out of? I didn't think so, but I didn't know for sure. I mean, I'd never been in the girls' room. What if there *was* a window, and Brianna climbed through it and got away while I was standing here dithering? The Grandfatherly One would be gone, and it would be all my fault!

I had to go in. Taking a deep breath, I pushed open the door and boldly went where no Tim had ever gone before.

Well, semiboldly. The first thing I did was slip out of those squeaky sneakers. I didn't want to spook Brianna into doing anything that might damage the Grandfatherly One. Given the alien technology, I figured his carrying case was probably pretty solid. But I couldn't be sure, and I didn't want to take any chances.

I managed to get in without making any noise.

The entryway was set up the same way it is for the boys' room—that is, when you first enter, there's a kind of baffle to keep anyone who's standing outside from looking into the room.

I stopped behind the baffle to listen.

I could hear Brianna's voice, but it was muffled, and I couldn't make out the words. Dropping to the floor again (I was spending a lot of time on the floor today!), I poked my head around the barrier.

The first thing I noticed was that the girls' room looks different from the boys' room. It took me a minute to realize what was missing. (Hint: It's where the boys stand when they don't need to sit.) Also, there were more stalls than in the boys' room—which makes sense if you figure that's what everyone has to use, every time.

Since I still couldn't see Brianna I figured she must be *in* one of those stalls.

Well, no need to stand up at this point. I just slithered forward on my belly until I spotted her feet.

From my new position I could hear her more clearly. "Sir, if you could just answer a few questions, I'd appreciate it very much."

"Who are you?" asked the Grandfatherly One.

"My name is Brianna Sawyer. I'm in Pleskit's class."

"Oh, yeah—I noticed you earlier. Come here, let me get a closer look at you."

I could hear Brianna step forward—and imagined the Grandfatherly One's vision tubes stretching out for a closer look. All of a sudden I heard him exclaim, "Great jumping galaxies!"

"Something wrong?" asked Brianna innocently.

"What's going on here?" demanded the Grandfatherly One. "What are you doing messing around with those kids?"

"What do you mean?"

"Come on, lady, you can't fool me."

Lady? What was he talking about?

"Look, Toots, I've been around the galaxy a time or two. Things may differ from planet to planet, but it's easy enough for me to see that you're no standard-issue sixth grader."

Brianna laughed, a sound that squeezed my heart. "All right, you've got me. I'm not really a sixth grader."

"Then what are you?"

I knew the answer even before she spoke—knew it, and hated it, and wanted to die of embarrassment.

"I'm a reporter."

A reporter! I had fallen in love with an older woman!

What was my mother going to say when she heard about this one?

"Clever thing, aren't you?" said the Grandfatherly One with a chuckle.

"I like to think so. Now what do you say—will you answer a few questions for me?"

"No, I don't think so. I want to go back to the classroom now."

"I'm afraid that won't be possible," said Brianna. She sounded almost sad.

"What is this?" asked the Grandfatherly One suspiciously. "A kidnapping?"

"Oh, let's not be so negative. I just need you to answer a few questions for me." To my surprise, Brianna's voice sounded desperate, almost fearful.

"What's the big deal, Toots?"

Her voice grew hard, cold. "Look, old man—just answer the questions and I'll get out of your face for good. Vanish. Scramboodle. If you won't, I'm going to have to figure out some way to take you with me."

"Is that a threat?"

"Take it however you want, Pops."

"I do not respond well to threats."

"Listen, you bodiless alien geezer. Answer the questions or—"

I had heard enough. I stood up and pushed on the door of the stall.

It wouldn't open.

So I kicked it in.

CHAPTER 18

[PLESKIT]
INTUITION

"ATTENTION! ATTENTION! All students and faculty are urgently requested to look for a purple carrying case containing the brain of Pleskit Meenom's Grandfatherly One. If anyone has the case in his or her room, please bring it to the office immediately."

While Principal Grand's voice boomed out over the loudspeaker, McNally was organizing the security guards into three search teams. I could hear him discussing how they would divide up the building and who would go where.

As soon as he put down the microphone, Mr. Grand said, "Ms. Blossom! Go classroom to classroom.

Tell the teachers to turn things upside down looking for that brain!"

"Aye-aye, sir!" said Ms. Blossom. Then she gave him a salute and left the office. I couldn't tell if she was making fun of him or not. From the look on his face, neither could he.

"This is all good," I said. "But what if the carrying case is already gone? *What if whoever took it has left the building?*"

"Security is too tight for that," said one of the guards.

McNally snorted. "Security is tight for people getting *in*. Getting *out* is no big deal."

From the look on the guard's face, I could see that this was true.

"Start looking!" cried Principal Grand. "We can't let a little thing like that stop us! Meenom will be here before long. Failure is not an option!"

The guards raced off in different directions. McNally went out to supervise the hunt. I was alone in the office, with only my fear and my guilt to keep me company. Fear, guilt, and a nagging suspicion at the back of my brain that I had overlooked something important—something that might be a key to the situation.

One of the things we learn early on Hevi-Hevi is that most of us are smarter than we think we are, know more than we think we know. On Earth they speak of something called "intuition"—a kind of mysterious knowing that cannot be explained. We, too, believe in this kind of knowing. But we think there *is* an explanation. We believe it comes from the brain working at the subconscious level, putting together things we have seen without realizing that we're seeing them. The hungry brain gathers information, and every once in a while sends us a message when we least expect it.

The reason I mention all this is to try to explain why, when I went out into the hall and saw a pair of sneakers in front of the girls' room, I suddenly knew I had to go inside. I could not have told you why this was so. But my brain insisted it was important.

Unfortunately Ms. Feinbacher's third grade was coming down the hall that very minute, heading for art class. I did not want to go barging into the girls' room in front of twenty-five third graders. But my intuition was screaming at me that I had to check out the situation.

Leaping in front of them, I held up one hand. My voice was soft but intense, I said, "Danger! Beware! I must request your silence!"

Before they could ask any questions, I pushed open the door and stepped silently into the girls' room. I stopped behind the visual barrier, listening carefully, hoping to gather new information.

I learned more than I'd expected.

Tim was speaking. "Who are you, and what are you doing with this brain?" he asked angrily.

I felt a thrill. The Grandfatherly One was here!

The voice that answered Tim belonged to Brianna Sawyer. Only it sounded huskier than usual. "I'm just trying to get a story, Timmy."

"Like all the other stories you got? The ones you sent to *The National News* and let me take the blame for? How could you do that to me?"

"Oh, don't be mad, sweetie. You don't mind taking a little flak on my behalf, do you?"

"I sure do," said Tim. "Especially when it costs me my best friend!"

Brianna laughed. "Silly Tim. If Pleskit were really

your friend, he wouldn't have been so easily taken in by that self-important little twit Jordan."

Grief and embarrassment twisted my *gnorzle*. How could I have been so blind?

I felt a little better—but only a little—when I heard the Grandfatherly One say, "Don't be so self-serving, lady. You set Tim up for a fall. True, my grandchildling fell for it more easily than he should have. But don't try to paint yourself as such a sweet little innocent."

"I'm not at all innocent," said Brianna. "But I do have a job to do. All I really want is an exclusive interview with you, Gramps. Don't stand in my way, Tim, and I'll even cut you in on this. It could be worth a lot of money. A *lot*. I've done my homework, kid; I know you and your mom don't have that much. She's got a lot of bills. We're talking the kind of money that can get you out of debt, out of that crummy apartment—out of this school if you want. A whole new life."

I pressed against the wall, breathlessly listening.

Tim said nothing.

Brianna's voice got softer, more intimate. "Even better, we're talking career here, Tim. This will be one of the biggest scoops in history. When you grow up, you could get a job with any news organization in the country. You'd be set for life."

"So I can be just like you?" asked Tim bitterly. "No, thanks, lady. Look, Pleskit is my friend. Well, he may not be my friend at the moment. But I'm still *his* friend. And I'm not going to betray him for some bloodsucker like you. Come on, we're taking that brain back where it belongs."

"Sorry, Tim," said Brianna, sounding a little desperate. "That's not part of the program. If you don't want to help, that's all right. I'll be out that window with the brain box in just a minute. But I can't let you sound the alarm. So I hope you'll forgive me, but—"

I heard a spraying sound, and then a thump—the sound of Tim's body hitting the floor.

"Help!" cried the Grandfatherly One. "Police! Forces of Justice! Any—"

Then his voice was muffled.

CHAPTER 19

[TIM]

RECONNECTION

Whatever was in the spray can Brianna pulled out of her pocket, it sure knocked me for a loop. The instant she spritzed it in my direction, I felt my knees wobble and my muscles go limp. A second later I was lying on the floor, staring at the ceiling. I was still wide awake—just totally unable to move.

Terror seized me. I had never heard of a spray that could paralyze you like this. Would it wear off? Or was I going to be stuck like this forever?

I wanted to scream, only I couldn't, because I didn't have control of a single muscle. This made me want to scream even more!

My brain felt like it was starting to itch. I wanted to explode from the frustration. I figured Brianna would escape with the Grandfatherly One, and I would be found lying on the girls' room floor . . . at which point everyone would decide I was not just a weirdo but a pervert as well.

A pervert who couldn't move.

Suddenly I heard Pleskit come roaring around the sight barrier. "Put down that brain, you evil vixen!" he shouted.

Brianna laughed and gave him a spritz with her spray can.

"Don't try that stuff on me," said Pleskit firmly. Then I heard a crackling sound. Sparkling light flickered against the ceiling. Brianna cried out, then (from the sound of it) slumped to the floor.

Pleskit must have zapped her with his *sphen-gnutksher*, just like he had done to Jordan on the second day of school!

"Grmble! Grmmph, gemph, mmrrmm!" said the Grandfatherly One.

"A moment, please," said Pleskit with a groan. "When

I have recovered I will untie your speaking tubes, O Venerated One."

I remembered that when Pleskit zapped someone, the blast sucked out all his own energy for a few minutes. So I knew he was okay, just waiting for the effect of the blast to wear off.

I couldn't see the scene, of course. But I could imagine it. I knew Brianna must be in what the Hevi-Hevians call *kling-kphut*, a blissful state of semiconsciousness where she would not be able to move for a while. Pleskit was either on his knees or on his back, waiting for his *sphen-gnut-ksher* to gather some more energy. And the Grandfatherly One's BTD was sitting nearby, the speaking tubes crossed in a knot that muffled anything he tried to say.

In short, everyone in the room was temporarily disabled.

Suddenly the door burst open. "Pleskit!" cried McNally. "Pleskit, are you in here?"

"Over here," said Pleskit, his voice weak.

McNally came around the barrier. "What the—"

"I'm fine," said Pleskit softly. "Just a little tired. You

had best see to my friend, Tim. I do not know what Brianna sprayed him with, but the effect was serious. I hope he will be all right."

McNally knelt over me. "Tim! Tim, you okay, kiddo?"

I wanted to answer but my tongue—like every other muscle in my body—had no interest in working. So I stayed silent.

McNally shook me. *"Tim!"*

I still didn't answer.

He pressed his ear to my chest. "He's breathing," he muttered. "Good heartbeat. Tim, I think you're gonna be okay, buddy. You *capisce*?"

I said nothing.

"I'll be back in a minute," said McNally. He turned to Pleskit. "What's been going on in here?"

"Untie the Grandfatherly One's speaker tubes," said Pleskit, his voice still weak. "He will explain."

"Ah, that's better!" said the Grandfatherly One a moment later. "Well done, kiddo. You, too, Tim—assuming you can hear me." Then he launched into an explanation of everything that had happened.

"You scum-sucking sidewinder," said McNally,

obviously speaking to Brianna. "I can't believe I was taken in by your kid act."

"Do not berate yourself on that account, McNally," said the Grandfatherly One. "I was fooled at first myself. Most species have a wide range as regards the age/appearance matrix. This deceptively juvenile-looking female probably had a terrible time in high school because everyone thought she was younger than she really was. That does not, of course, excuse her current treachery."

"Terrible time," murmured Brianna dreamily, which was our first sign that the *kling-kphut* was wearing off.

"All right, lady," said McNally, and I got the impression he was kneeling next to her, shaking her. "Spill. What was that stuff you used on Tim?"

"Stuff," murmured Brianna. "Nice stuff make Tim fall down."

McNally made a sound of disgust. "How much longer before she's able to talk normally?"

"Probably another five minutes," said Pleskit. "As for me, I am feeling considerably better. Let us leave this room of personal functions and alert Mr.

Grand and the guards to what has occurred."

"Good idea," said McNally. "But Tim's going out on a stretcher. I want to be careful of him. Let me get the nurse. I'll be right back."

It wasn't long before I was lying on the bed in the nurse's office. And it wasn't long after that when Pleskit came in and sprayed something in my face.

I coughed and blinked. Suddenly my whole body was tingling with a pins-and-needles feeling. It was like when your foot goes to sleep, except it was everywhere.

"Yow!" I cried, sitting up. "What did you just do?"

"Sprayed you with the antidote," said Pleskit. "Brianna had it in her backpack." He looked very serious. "This spray was not of Earthly origin, Tim. I fear my enemies may be more numerous and more powerful than I realized."

I shook myself several times, the way you do when a chill runs down your spine. "Brrrrrr! What a weird feeling."

"Are you all right?" asked Pleskit, sitting down beside me.

I shook my head and blinked a couple of times. "I think so. Did your Fatherly One get here yet?"

Pleskit smiled. "He will be here soon. It is good of you to be concerned, especially after . . . well, after all that has happened. I am sorry that I doubted you, Tim."

I wanted to say, "Hey, don't worry about it." But even though I wanted more than anything to be friends, the words seemed to stick in my throat. I was still angry and hurt.

"Please," said Pleskit. "Can we be friends again?"

I remembered what Linnsy had said to me when I asked her advice earlier, and how I had ignored her.

I *should* have said something then.

I *had* to say something now.

"Sure," I said. "Hands across the stars?"

"Hands across the stars," said Pleskit.

We shook on it.

CHAPTER 20

[PLESKIT]
A LETTER HOME

FROM: Pleskit Meenom, on the strange but interesting Planet Earth
TO: Maktel Geebrit, on the beautiful but distant Planet Hevi-Hevi

Dear Maktel:

Well, that's it. I hope you will not be too disturbed that my friendship with Tim has become such an important thing to me. One of the things I figured out from this whole mess was that there is room in the *smorgle* for more than one, that one friend need not displace another.

As to what happened after we recovered

the Grandfatherly One's brain from the evil Brianna—well, once again luck was with me. I might have been in a great deal of trouble with the Fatherly One (a horrifying amount of trouble, actually), but the Grandfatherly One stepped in (as much as a disembodied brain can step anywhere) and bawled out the Fatherly One for not paying more attention to him. He claimed to be utterly satisfied at having been out in the world and having had "a lovely little adventure"—which is not exactly how I would describe such a terrifying incident, but I was staying quiet at that moment.

Now I must tell you the strange, dark side of how things resolved. As I told Tim, it was clear that the spray Brianna used on him was not a standard Earthling device. When McNally questioned her about where she got it, she said, "The Boss gave it to me."

But she claimed she didn't know who "The Boss" was, and nothing they could do would shake her from that story. McNally questioned her for a long time, and then consulted with the Fatherly One for an equally long time. We are almost certain that "The Boss" is another extraterrestrial trying to sabotage the Fatherly One's mission.

Sometimes I wish we could just go home. But it is not simply that the Fatherly One has a chance to make our fortune here. We have both—we admitted it to each other—become fond of the Earthlings. And we do not want to leave them unprotected from some of the other characters that might move in if we abandon our Trading Claim. Little do the Earthlings realize how important it is to them that our mission succeed; little do they realize what the alternatives are.

Well, enough of that. The embassy is in the grip of nervous excitement even as I am writing this. Tomorrow, at last, Beezle Whompis will be arriving. I cannot wait to meet the Fatherly One's new assistant. I deeply hope that this being will be more pleasant to deal with than the dreaded Ms. Buttsman.

Tim has asked me to tell you hello. Like me,

he is hoping you will come and visit sometime.

I think you will like him.

I know I do.

Please write soon.

Fremmix Bleeblom!

Your pal,

Pleskit

CHAPTER 21

[MAKTEL] A LETTER TO EARTH

FROM: Maktel Geebrit, on Planet Hevi-Hevi
TO: Pleskit Meenom, on Planet Earth

Dear Pleskit:

Thanks for your latest missive. I love hearing about your weird adventures on that primitive planet.

Listen, I don't have much time now, but I have to give you two pieces of news, one good, one bad.

If I remember correctly, you always prefer to get the bad news first, so you can use the good news to make you feel better.

Okay, here's the bad stuff. Yestereve my

parental unit hosted a small gathering, a dinner party attended by three other beings.

As you know, if you press a *mizrick* shell to the floor of my sleeping chamber, it is possible to hear most of what is going on in the dining room below. Normally the adult conversation is too boring to bother with doing this. However, after the group had been quite boisterous for some time, their voices suddenly grew hushed and low—always a sign that something worth listening to is being said.

So I got out my *mizrick* shell.

They were talking about your Fatherly One and his mission! Pleskit, things do not look good. Erglom Benzwemp, who is my Motherly One's special friend, believes there are *several* other traders on Earth, all secretly trying to undermine your Fatherly One's mission. Erglom also says that your Fatherly One has enemies in the High Council. Caution is advised!

Well, there it is. Pretty nasty, I'm sure you will agree.

Now for the good news. It is possible—just barely possible, but possible nonetheless—that I might be able to visit Earth in time to celebrate our Hatching Day! What a treat it would be to meet your weird new friends and see the strange and barbaric places you have been telling me about!

I am still working on the Motherly One, but things are looking good.

I cannot wait to see you again!

Yertyop jig,

Maktel

SPECIAL BONUS:

On the following pages you will find Part Three of *Disaster on Geembol Seven*—the story of what happened to Pleskit on the last planet where he lived before coming to Earth.

This story is being told in six installments, one at the end of each of the first six books of the Sixth-Grade Alien series. Look for the next thrilling chapter in Book Four, *Lunch Swap Disaster*!

DISASTER ON GEEMBOL SEVEN

PART THREE: THROUGH CAVERNS VAST AND DARKNESS DEEP

FROM: Pleskit Meenom, on Planet Earth
TO: Maktel Geebrit, on Planet Hevi-Hevi

Dear Maktel,

I sense I am taking longer than you would like to tell the full story of what happened on Geembol Seven. But between all the craziness here on Earth and the fact that the memory is still quite painful, it is not something I can do quickly.

Even so, here is the next part.

You will remember I had been on Geembol only a few days when the Fatherly One took me to the Moondance Celebration. While munching candied waterbugs, I spotted a six-eyed boy who clearly needed help. I followed him to the waterfront, where I was pulled into an elevator hidden inside one of the huge pilings that support the ancient docks. It took me deep into the planet. The being who had pulled me in was a "construct"—a strange (and illegal) combination of biological and mechanical parts—named Balteeri. He and the boy, whose name was Derrvan, wanted me to hear their story. I agreed, despite their warning that to listen was a crime. But before they could even begin, something terrifying burst through the wall. . . .

A horrible shrieking filled the cave. A blaze of harsh lights seared my vision. Derrvan flung up an arm to cover his face. As he staggered back, crying out in pain, I realized that, with six eyes, his pain must have been much greater than mine.

The pulsing green creatures that clung to the cavern's ceiling pulled in their tentacles and flattened themselves against the stone. If they made any sound of protest or pain, it was lost in the evil blare of the sirens.

Half blinded by the sudden light, I could get only partial images of the invading machines. I did see huge drills at the front, spitting stone and sand as they whirled. Suddenly Balteeri grabbed me with one of his metallic arms and slammed me into the elevator that had brought us down here. I felt Derrvan jammed in beside me. An instant later Balteeri was inside, too. The door slid shut. After the glaring lights, the darkness seemed more complete than ever, though it was a welcome relief.

The elevator started to move. To my surprise, we were heading down again. How deep into the planet were we going to go?

"What was that all about?" I asked. My voice sounded small and frightened, which bothered me. On the other hand, fear was not unreasonable, given the circumstances.

"The law units are after us," replied Balteeri grimly.

A moment later the elevator stopped so abruptly that it nearly relocated my *clinkus*.

"Out!" ordered Balteeri. *"Out!"*

Then, as if not trusting us to do what he said quickly enough, he pulled Derrvan and me out of the elevator. (Despite the fact that it was blacker than a *catwump's* heart, I knew he pulled both of us because I heard Derrvan's gasp and felt him bump against me.)

"Where are we going?" I asked.

"No time to talk!" snapped Balteeri.

One of his mechanical additions began to glow. He kept the light low, so as not to blind us after the intense blackness. We were in a broad tunnel. Not far ahead sat something that looked like a small spaceship—an odd thing to find so far underground.

"Climb in!" ordered Balteeri. He must have been carrying some remote control device, because as he spoke, the top of the vehicle opened. He vaulted in. Derrvan followed, scrambling up the side.

I thought briefly about resisting but feared

if I did they would leave me. Then what would I do? I had no certainty that I could work the elevator. In fact, the pursuers might even have destroyed the shaft, in which case I would be trapped in this deep, dark place forever.

I climbed into the vehicle.

The interior space held the three of us comfortably, though it would have been crowded with even one additional passenger. A restraining strap closed over me as I settled into my seat.

Two of Balteeri's mechanical arms reached forward to link with the control panel. The ship slid into motion. At the same time a set of headlights came on. Through the view panel I could see that the cavern stretched a long way ahead of us. The path, however, was not a clear one; fanglike stone formations sprouted from the floor and stretched down from the ceiling. In some places they had fused to make complete columns.

I hoped Balteeri wasn't planning on going too fast.

That hope evaporated almost instantly. The ship shot forward, and I gasped with fear as we began zipping around the treacherous shafts of stone. But Balteeri was justified in his speed. Seconds later there was a glare of light from behind us, and a magnified voice roared, "STOP! STOP THIS INSTANT!"

"Suck stone, scumface," muttered Balteeri. A savage look twisted his face as he increased our speed.

Fearing I was about to go into *kleptra*, I reached out to clutch something for support. What I grabbed turned out to be Derrvan. I glanced at him. His face showed the same terror that I felt. Yet he looked excited, too. And angry.

As I said, you can express a lot with six eyes.

We were moving so fast the stone pillars were little more than a blur.

"Does this tunnel go anywhere?" I asked nervously. I was trying to fight back an image of us ending our journey by splattering against a solid stone wall.

"It used to," said Balteeri.

"Used to?" squeaked Derrvan.

Balteeri smiled grimly. "If luck is with us, it still does. But we've got to get clear before I dare take us there."

"Take us where?" demanded Derrvan. I was surprised by the tone of command in his voice.

"To the secret haven your father built for the constructs," replied Balteeri.

Derrvan gasped in surprise but said nothing more.

Balteeri raised our speed even further. The little ship lurched sickeningly as we dodged among the stony barriers. More than once Balteeri flipped us onto our side to hurtle through a narrow gap. It was only the restraining straps that kept Derrvan and me from slamming against the cabin wall.

Our pursuers began firing force beams. Their shots splattered against the rocks around us in bursts of multicolored light. Once I heard a roar of pain that sounded like rocks grinding together. A huge eye, round and yellow, opened in what I had thought was a boulder, and a paw the size of a small house snatched at us. Balteeri dodged it safely, but I heard the crunch of metal behind us.

"One down," said Balteeri happily. "Those fools should be careful where they shoot. *Nimtargs* don't like to be woken so rudely. Ah, here we go. Hold on!"

Suddenly we flipped sideways again and shot into a breathtakingly narrow passage—not that that slowed Balteeri down. After several terrifying minutes of watching stony walls that were far too close flash by in a blur, we burst out into an open area so vast that even with our ship's powerful lights we could not see any walls at all. If not for the fact that I knew there were twelve moons in the sky that night, I might have thought we were on the planet's surface again.

"Hold on," muttered Balteeri. He cut the lights, and darkness engulfed us. At the same time we began to plummet, dropping so fast I

felt like my middle parts were trying to push their way through the top of my head.

Our craft had a viewport in its roof. Looking up, I saw a shaft of light as our pursuers burst into the cavern. They raced straight ahead, unaware that we were now below them.

"Nicely done, Balteeri!" said Derrvan triumphantly.

We moved more slowly now, though still faster than seemed safe to me.

Deeper we went, and deeper still, until at last we came to another cavern—a place, I would soon learn, of sorrow and strangeness.

And it was here, at last, that Derrvan and Balteeri told me their story.

To be continued . . .

A GLOSSARY OF ALIEN TERMS

Following is a list of Hevi-Hevian words and phrases that appear for the first time in this book. (Words first used in Books One and Two of *Sixth-Grade Alien* can be found in the glossary at the end of Book Two: *I Shrank My Teacher.*)

The number after a definition indicates the chapter where the term first appears.

For most words here we are only giving the spelling. In actual usage many would, of course, be accompanied by smells or body sounds.

GEEZIL BEEDRUM: A slightly vulgar slang term used by kids on Hevi-Hevi. Literally translated it means "great boogers of doom." Not approved for use in polite company. (7)

GNORZLE: The internal organ where words are formed; located between the airsac and the swallow box (18)

GRAKKIMS: Fierce beach-dwelling creatures that like to build intricate sand structures. (6)

HERKLUMP: A heavily armored herdbeast found in the equatorial plains of Hevi-Hevi. May reach weights in excess of four tons. Often referred to as "the largest animal known to exist without the benefit of a brain." (This is not true, of course. *Herklumps* do have brains, but no one knew it for a long time because a *herklump's* brain is [a] somewhat smaller than a grape and [b] located—for reasons no one quite understands—in its rear end.) (4)

MIZRICK: A tubular beach animal with a distinctive purple shell. The shells, which are beautiful and often brought home as vacation souvenirs, are famous for their sound-conducting qualities. (21)

SMORGLE: The portion of the Hevi-Hevian brain devoted to matters of love and friendship. (20)

SPRATZELS: Fierce beach-dwelling creatures that delight in tearing down intricate sand structures. (6)

SQUAMBUL: An underwater vine that grows in the northern ponds of Hevi-Hevi. When infected with *perzink* (a moldlike substance), its roots develop large, tasty pods that are highly nutritious. A favorite snack food on Hevi-Hevi. Exported throughout the galaxy. (10)

VERPLEXXIM: Unpleasant and tense. The term comes from the phrase *"Agle agbit* <tiny fart> [angry smell] *eskbat eegle verplexxim"* (literally: "I have an *agbit* thorn under the skin of my butt, and it is making me totally miserable." This was a common problem for early workers in the wampfields, and though it no longer actually happens, the term has entered popular use). (6)

WUNGBORKLE: A snakelike creature found in the swamps of Mingbat Seven. *Wungborkles* can reach a length of up to fifty feet and have anywhere between two and eight hands. (Hands are highly prized, and the more hands a *wungborkle* can grow, the greater its prestige.) They are highly intelligent, and highly vicious. Their skins, which they shed on a regular basis, are greatly prized by fashion designers around the galaxy. (13)

ZARKAFLIAN SHLNUTBERG: A hard-shelled creature that dwells in the ice fields of Zarkafle (fourth planet out from the star Mixtorpia). Eight to ten inches long when fully grown, the *shlnutberg* is a particularly dangerous parasite because it sucks the warmth out of other creatures. Early explorers to the ice fields often froze to death when attacked by groups of *shlnutbergs.* (4)